THE WINDOW OF THE HO

THE WINDOW OF THE HOUSE OPPOSITE

by
Govinda Bahadur Malla *"Gothale"*

Translated from the Nepali by
Larry Hartsell

This translation was made possible by a grant from the National Endowment for the Arts, USA.

BOOK FAITH INDIA
Delhi

THE WINDOW OF THE HOUSE OPPOSITE
Translated from the Nepali by Larry Hartsell

Published by
BOOK FAITH INDIA
414-416 Express Tower, Azadpur Commercial Complex
Delhi, India 110 033

Distributed by
PILGRIMS BOOK HOUSE
P.O. Box 3872, Kathmandu, Nepal
P.O. Box 38, Varanasi, India
Tel: 977-1-424942, 425919
Fax: 977-1-424943. E-mail: info@pilgrims.wlink.com.np

Layout & Cover Design by Sherap Sherpa

Cover Photograph Courtesy Larry Hartsell

1st English Edition

Printed in India
at Gopsons Papers Ltd., NOIDA

Translator's dedication

For Raymond

TABLE OF CONTENTS

Foreword

Born in an upper class Newar family of Kathmandu, Govinda Bahadur Malla "Gothale" spent most of his childhood with his Rana playmates in one or the other of their palaces that dotted the capital. We can trace his royal descent from the Malla kings of Bhaktapur, a city-state in the not very distant past. His house was a hub of intellectual and literary activities. His father Riddhi Bahadur Malla edited and published *Sharada,* the only prestigious literary journal to appear during the Rana regime in the country, in the thirties and forties. All this background naturally equipped the talented young man "Gothale" to write brilliant prose plays delineating the Rana rulers and their slow decay with much insight into upper class characters in Nepal. In his fiction, however, "Gothale" presents a penetrating vision of lower middle class Newars who were his immediate neighbours, and with whom he had to deal every day while assisting his father in running the Jore Ganesh Press and several other publications including *Sharada.*

Famous personalities of Nepali literature like Laxmi Prasad Devkota, Bal Krishna Sama and Lekha Nath Paudyal frequented his father's living room, but he made his models young and energetic Dramatist Gopal Prasad Rimal and short story writers Bishweshwar Prasad Koirala and Bhawani Bhikshu were very close to him. Rimal was a social realist while Koirala and Bhikshu had introduced psychoanalysis in their stories. "Gothale" adopted the psychoanalytical method and applied it very successfully to both his plays and short stories.

The Window of the House Opposite began as a short story, but as it progressed the writer did not feel that he could do full justice to Misri, the main female character, if he abruptly ended the narration for the sake of producing a short story. Technically the author tried to restrict his emotional flow, but the finished product was an unusually beautiful novella admired and welcomed in the literary world of the country. The novella is a masterpiece of Nepali fiction with its local touches and brilliant illumination of human weaknesses.

Larry Hartsell has, as in his former translations, brought this short novel to English readers with most of the Nepali nuances conveyed accurately and successfully.

January 15, 1998
Taranath Sharma

Chapter One

LIGHT filtered in through the cracks and crevices of the closed door and windows so that every object was becoming distinct. For a moment the light fell upon young Misri's head and rested there. Misri smiled a little in her sleep.

The sound of someone saying "Watch out! I'm coming up!" filled the house, piercing the chattering of the sparrows. Misri's mother was climbing the narrow stairs, carrying fresh water. Misri slowly opened her eyes to the voice of her mother. The smile dancing on her face disappeared. Surprised, she looked all around, and felt that her dream was real, waking life a lie.

"Eh! It's morning. I have to get up!" she thought, and made some effort to get out of bed. But she couldn't get up, couldn't face the cold outside her bed.

"This really is my parents' house," she thought, and again closed her eyes. She tried to bring the smile back to her face. She dreamed briefly, and then forgot what she had dreamed immediately, as the dream played hide-and-seek in her brain and she couldn't capture it. Just then, from the kitchen above came the sound of a pot falling, and she opened her eyes again.

She still couldn't leave her quilt. "This is my parents' house—no need to hurry," she thought, closing her eyes. Then all at once she threw aside the covers and abruptly got up. Yes, this was her parents' house, but there was also her husband's house; there was also her husband.

Misri sat up and gazed at the crumpled-up quilt for some time. "There was her husband's house, there was also her husband." Without folding the quilt she slowly made her way to the window. When she opened the window shutters, the room filled with light, and the cool air touched her cheek—and then her eyes automatically came to rest on the house opposite. The sun was shining on the roof of that house and light, thin fog covered the lower portion. Her eyes moved leisurely downwards, halting at a window in the lowest story. That window looked silent, as if hiding a profound mystery in the midst of the fog. After some time, it seemed that a man's form was moving about in that window. She rapidly moved her eyes back up to the roof.

"No, that man only comes to the house at three or four o'clock." Misri again lowered her eyes. Now it seemed as if someone had pulled back the curtains—yes, someone had indeed pulled back the curtains. Misri quickly closed the window shutters. She leaned against the closed shutters for some time. She slowly moved away and picked up the quilt, folded it, and put it on a corner of the bed.

She was to leave for her own home in four days. She had stayed in her parents' house for a month. "How quickly a month has gone by," she sighed, and counted the remaining days on her fingers. "Friday, Saturday, Sunday, Monday."

If Misri didn't want to go, her mother would say, "Good! Don't go!" She stopped counting abruptly. What excuse was there for saying she wouldn't go? After a moment she came back to reality. "What if mother knew what I was thinking? Anyway, what have I done?" she imagined arguing. "Can't I go into my own bedroom? Can't I look out my own window? How is it my fault if someone is watching me from over there? Even if degenerates from all over the whole city are staring, what have I done wrong? No one can accuse me of anything!"

"These hoodlums are disgusting!" she muttered, as she went to the window. "What interest could I have in that house? This is my house, and who's to stop me from opening my own window?"

She opened the window shutters, and the room again filled with light. The fog had completely lifted from the house opposite, and sunlight had reached the attic floor.

"I opened the window. So?" She looked about, and picked up a broom. "I'll do some sweeping. If someone were to see me, what fault do I have?"

Misri started to sweep the room.

After she finished sweeping, the room fell silent. It seemed to Misri that the whole house was silent, that everything was silent. The sound of a baby crying came from upstairs. She left her room, went up the stairs, and approached the door of the kitchen. The baby was shrieking. The kitchen was filled with suffocating smoke, and her sister-in-law was rinsing the uncooked rice. The fire had gone out in the hearth, and smoke was pouring forth. On one side the baby, who had been put aside, was crying and waving its arms and legs. The three-year-old was tugging at his mother's shawl and whining for *chiura*-pounded rice. "*Chiura, chiura*!" Misri fled the room and stood on the stair.

She thought, "It's my parents' house; I came here to rest a few days." At the same time a thought suddenly occurred to her: "I have a husband. There is my husband's house."

She turned around and entered the kitchen again. Her sister-in-law looked askance at her, but in her eyes there was no begging, no humility, no plea for help. She only looked, and slapped the boy whining for *chiura*. Now the boy, too, began to cry. The kitchen, completely filled with smoke, was also filled with the crying of the two children. Misri's brain was reeling. Even though she felt a strong urge to flee the room, she stayed. After a moment, she advanced slowly, somewhat ashamed, somewhat abashed. Her sister-in-law watched her come in. But in her sister-in-law's eyes there was no begging, no humility.

Misri said, "Why are you whining? Hush!" The boy would not calm down, and her sister-in-law said nothing. She was so fed up with the pandemonium she could not speak. Misri picked up the smaller crying baby and rocked him next to her breast. She exclaimed, "What a lot of smoke there is!"

The baby she had clasped to her breast stopped crying and searched for her nipple. It tickled her, and she smiled as she looked at the infant. She said, "With so much smoke, it's no wonder the baby cries so much!"

The sobbing little boy left the kitchen.

Her sister-in-law glanced at her for a moment. Sister-in-law wanted to say something, didn't, but then suddenly spoke. "*You* tell me—what can I do? I have to do everything myself. I don't have a moment's peace from the time I get up to the time I go to sleep. These kids—who won't do me the favor of dropping dead—always pester me like this. Your younger brother has to go to school at ten o'clock, and your older brother comes home for a meal at twelve. And it's just fine for some people to be at their prayers until twelve o'clock!"

How could her sister-in-law say such a thing about her mother—how could she have the nerve? Misri watched her sister-in-law. "Am I not the only person working in the house? To me..." Her complaint stopped abruptly. "She..." Misri became lost in thought: I have a husband. There is my husband's house.

The baby shrieked and again began to cry. The sound of crying pierced her entire body. She bared her teeth, and hissed breathlessly, "I said, be quiet!"

She took the baby upstairs. Her mother was busy at prayer in the *puja* room, next to the roof verandah. Her mother did not speak, but her eyes asked, "What?"

Misri retreated from there as well. The baby had stopped crying. Misri went to the lowest floor and stood next to her father's room. The voice of her father, Dhan Prasad, sounded from inside the room. "Who is it? Misri?"

Misri said, "It's me!"

"What is it?"

"Nothing."

"What is your mother doing?"

"*Puja*."

"Oh! She's doing her *puja*? Here, I... Bring me a little water."

Her older brother was coming up the stairs at the same time she was coming up to get some water. She abruptly handed the baby to her brother and continued upstairs.

Her brother called out, "Hey, why did you give this to me? I'm on my way out!"

Climbing on up the stairs, Misri said, "Go out, do whatever you want. Sister-in-law..."

She stopped and looked at her brother's face. Here was her brother, the husband of her sister-in-law. As she climbed the stairs, it seemed that her feet would stick on every step. I have a husband. There is my husband's house.

When she went into the kitchen to get her father some water, her sister-in-law gazed at her again. In her sister-in-law's eyes, there was no begging, no humility. Those eyes were so emotionless, and so firm. Misri was so jarred by this that she absently stirred the dipper back and forth in the water pot for some time.

"What are you doing? Isn't there any water in the water pot?" her sister-in-law asked.

"There is," Misri said in a soft voice, and looked pleadingly at her sister-in-law, but at that time her sister-in-law was looking toward the hearth. Misri awoke from her trance, scooped some water out of the pot, and went out. As she descended the stairs, again her feet seemed to stick on each step. As she set the water pitcher down in front of her father, she stood confusedly among the furnishings.

"What are you looking for?" her father asked.

"Nothing!" she said in a soft voice, and left the room. Then, on the verandah, she felt very tired. She thought, "I feel so sleepy."

She went to lean against the edge of the verandah, and gazed for some time into the distance. The clouds concealing the peaks were gradually melting away. From among the rooftops a temple secretly raised its head, a head exceedingly mute and firm. At that moment, her mother suddenly rang the bell in the *puja* room. With the sound of the bell, it seemed to Misri that the rooftops of the houses, piled against one another, mingled with the mountain tops, one pushing against the other, and all were jumbled up in the clouds. She sat down.

She sat for a long time, doing nothing. It seemed to her that her feet were stuck to the floor, that some weight was pressing on her head. She couldn't stand up.

She wanted to escape from that suffocating place; she wanted to free herself by throwing aside the obstacles that entangled her feet and weighed her down. She wanted to be free of worry. Misri got up suddenly and went downstairs. She wanted, untroubled, to help her sister-in-law in the kitchen. She went there, but her sister-in-law had the same eyes as before, in which there was no begging, no humility. What work could she do? Without settling on anything, she leaned against the window and watched her sister-in-law work. She felt how helpless and idle she was every day. The rice was sputtering in the pot. Light smoke filled the kitchen, and her eyes filled with tears. She didn't know if those tears were the result of the smoke, or of her own unhappiness. Again she got up abruptly, wanting to run away and be free of that suffocating place.

But when she came near the stairs she felt overpowered, and sat down. She felt extremely sleepy—really, she wanted to rid herself of these problems within her, smooth them over with sleep. She said to herself again, "I'm so tired!"

But she didn't have the courage to go into her own bedroom. Just opposite that room was the house that man frequented. She wanted to cry out: "That man is a hoodlum, a troublemaker!"

Misri wanted to say to that hoodlum's face, "Who do you think you are, to look at me as if you would gobble me up!"

But Misri would be in her bedroom sitting by the window when that fair-skinned young man-about-town appeared in the street, wearing fashionable clothes. That man would look up toward the window in which she was sitting. His eyes would be smiling, his whole body would be smiling, and as he went into the house opposite he would cry out, "Ramman! Ramman!"

At that time Misri would be watching from her window, and she would be sitting in a place from which she could watch, a place where she could not be seen by the people in the house opposite. All day long the sun would be shining on that house. The sun would have been up for a long time, would be shining in the windows of the lowest floor in which their neighbor Ramman lived. Then those silhouettes, the forms of those men, would hang around loafing. The eyes of that man would search for Misri in the house opposite. In that room they would play cards and carom, and the jokes and gossip would echo to her room, carried on a breeze. Every day it would be the same—that man would come, look up, call to her neighbor Ramman. And in the room the forms of those men would dance. The eyes of that man would search for her, and the echo of jokes and gossip would reach her on the wings of a breeze.

But along with all that, from somewhere, from everywhere in the room, from every corner, the two eyes of Misri's husband would be watching her steadily. Those two eyes would be watching patiently from his thin face. Her husband's eyes watched her like a baby watching its mother. In those eyes there was no jealousy, there was no pleading. In her husband's house, while she was sweeping the floor those eyes watched her. While she was cooking rice in the kitchen those eyes would be fixed on her from the interior window, watching her. It made her uneasy—exceedingly uneasy. When she and her husband were alone in the bedroom at night, those eyes smiled, but it seemed to Misri that her husband did not smile with his whole body. Her husband would go to the shop and bring home what was necessary, neither more nor less, watching her in the same way, which made her uneasy. When her husband emerged from the *puja* room after worshipping the gods, she felt uneasy. When he ate his meal, and didn't say whether it tasted good or not, didn't say anything, she felt uneasy. And when he finished eating his meal, fearing that his wife would go hungry, he urged her to bow down at his feet in the traditional greeting before he left for the office. At that time also, Misri felt uneasy.

Just then, as Misri was leaning on her elbow with her palm on her forehead, her mother called, "Misri!"

But her husband's silent eyes and the eyes of the man-about-town who comes to the house opposite were jumbled together. Her elbow suddenly slipped from her lap and made her palm fall from her forehead, giving her head a jolt.

Right then her mother called again. "Misri, did you hear?"

Suddenly she wanted to be released from that suffocating place, to get rid of those confusing thoughts and be free of them. She became alert and sat up straight.

"How many times have I called you?"

Misri looked at her mother. "What?"

"What's wrong?"

"Nothing."

Misri saw that her mother was looking at her with concern, and repeated. "Nothing's wrong—everything is all right."

"What's wrong? Do you have a headache? You look as if something is wrong," her mother said.

Misri laughed scornfully.

"What are you laughing about?" her mother said, pretending to get angry. Misri, restraining her anger, said, "Nothing is wrong! Nothing at all is wrong!"

Her mother, surprised, continued to look at her searchingly.

Misri suddenly felt as if she were boiling within, as if something had stuck in her throat. However, she tried to smile, and raised her eyes to look at her mother.

"What's happening in this house? I can't talk with anyone about anything without getting my head bit off!" said her mother.

Misri tried to say something, but before she could speak, her mother had reached the door of the room. Misri now completely forgot what she was trying to say. Now she wanted to force out the words that were stuck in her throat. She began to sob. After a moment, surprised at herself and a little ashamed, she became silent.

Her husband also had a mother who, like her own mother, was middle-aged. But what a difference there was between her mother and her mother-in-law! No matter what Misri did, no matter how much she was at fault, her mother loved her. When Misri saw her own mother, she felt no fear, but whenever she saw her mother-in-law, she always felt afraid. Her mother still looked young, but her mother-in-law was always gaunt and ill, and a hint of envy was always visible in her eyes. Misri sensed no compassion in her mother-in-law at all, whether she looked at Misri with anger, whether with love, or whether she merely spoke. It always seemed to Misri that her mother-in-law hated her, and she felt like concealing her whole body in some corner of her mind. She always had a feeling of suffocation. Even though her mother-in-law did not speak with a loud voice, her eyes always seemed about to give an order, and Misri kept searching for more work to do. Constantly working, Misri didn't have a moment's rest all day. If there were a moment's rest, her mother-in-law's eyes would look as if she were about to issue an order, and she would search and search for more work to be done. Even though Misri worked very hard, she still had to be cautious. That is, her mother-in-law could sniff out any rebellious deception, and master it. Again, her mother was not there, who would always say, "Do you have a headache?"

And then, even if Misri were ravenously hungry, she couldn't eat quickly when her mother-in-law gave her food. She had to pretend she didn't feel like eating. It was as if her mother-in-law were judging every movement of her hands and face, and Misri had to prove she was not a glutton. But here at home, her own mother always said, "Eat! Shall I give you some more?"

And whenever Misri looked at her own face in the mirror, she saw clearly that her face looked pitiable and defeated. Her two steady eyes did not smile now; they seemed to be pleading, "Please, please be kind to me." Suddenly it occurred to her that her face and the face of her husband looked the same. Her husband's eyes were small, his nose a little large and long, his cheeks a little hollow, but nonetheless their faces had the same look.

Misri gently began to massage her knees, as if she were gently soothing her husband's face as he lay with his head in her lap; she felt like gently massaging his head. Her husband had complete faith in Misri's love, as if she had taken birth solely to give him love. And her husband didn't seem to beg for love from her, just as she had no need to beg for love from her own mother, as if he had received love without begging for it, which was his right. Just as she had confidence and trust in her own mother's love, he likewise had trust in hers.

After she had eaten, Misri said to herself that she would not go into her bedroom all day, as long as that hoodlum remained in that house. If for some reason she did have to go there, she would not open the window shutters. Then that man would lose hope, and even if he came back tomorrow or the next day he would not dare look towards her.

"Yes, he will give up hope" she thought, savoring the idea. "Then he won't dare look this way. How nice that will be! That despicable face..."

She imagined that despicable, hopeless face, and smiled.

The day began to pass, and it seemed that some tension was building. Twelve o'clock, and after a bit 12:30. And then one o'clock. Her heart began to beat faster. Maybe that man had come to the house opposite! The beating of her heart counted the moments. And with that she felt anxious: shall I go look? Has he come or not? And how would that disappointed face look? A quarter past one. She saw it clearly in her imagination. That man would come and look up from the street. His smiling face would be downcast. He would slowly enter that house opposite, looking again and again to see if Misri might appear.

Misri wanted to know if this would happen in reality, but she didn't dare go to her own room. "Why doesn't Mother ask me to do some work in my room?" she thought. But there was no sign that her mother was near. Her mother could be upstairs doing something in the attic. Misri strained her ears to listen. Her mother did not make a sound. She looked all about, trying to think of an excuse to go to her room, but she couldn't think of any work to do there. After a moment, it suddenly occurred to her that she had to stitch up a blouse. As she started to get up, her eye fell on the opposite wall, where something surprised her. On top of the chest pushed against the wall, her blouse and the sewing materials seemed to taunt her. "Look! Here I am!" She realized she had brought them here yesterday. Then she calmed down and gave up. She decided that she would not go into her room.

She again examined her face in her mind's eye. It was as before, pitiable and defeated. Her face was like her husband's, and the feeling in the eyes the same. She gently lay her hand on her cheek. Her whole face was like that of her husband. She gently stroked her cheek—that is, she wanted to stroke her own face, just as she wanted to caress her husband.

She said to herself, "I won't go! I won't go there!"

"Yes, it is a sin," it was as if she heard someone sigh.

"Sin!" As if to understand the meaning of the word, Misri repeated it to herself. "Sin!"

She stood up abruptly when the meaning of sin actually sank in. For some time she paced back and forth in the room. She reminded herself that no, she hadn't committed a sin, the sin was not even in her mind. She thought of her husband, how loving he was, and how much he cared for her. For a long time her husband's eyes appeared, filled with confidence and trust. As that loving pitiable face appeared before her, Misri sat down and sighed, "I didn't commit any sin!"

A human shape had stopped and was standing in front of the door to the room. It seemed to Misri that this shape had been there for a long time. She slowly lifted her eyes. Her sister-in-law, carrying the sleeping baby, was watching her.

Her sister-in-law said, "I wondered who was in the room."

Misri was gripped with doubt, and lowered her eyes.

"Were you sleeping?"

But Misri said nothing. She only shook her head, which could have meant yes or no.

Her sister-in-law spoke briefly about this and that, then she left, and Misri immediately remembered what her sister-in-law had said several days before.

"That man is always looking at this house." Her sister-in-law had looked at her sharply and said, "He looks as if he's thinking 'what can I get there?'"

At that time, Misri was in a happy mood and, noting the tenor of her sister-in-law's voice and face, she laughed. When Sister-in-law said, "That hoodlum keeps mistresses outside somewhere, and causes his wife no end of suffering," a kind of twisted brightness came into Misri's eyes. Her sister-in-law sighed, and said, "With people like that around, it's difficult to walk in the streets. It's too frightening." And Misri, to tease her, said, "What would you do if my brother got a mistress?"

Her sister-in-law pretended to be angry and said, "I'd lock your brother out of my room, then I'd throw him out by the scruff of the neck, and then he could go to his woman!"

Later, Misri said, "men are like that. No matter how wonderful a man's wife, he will still go after other women. Men are like that!"

"Yes, that man is no good!" said Misri, and raised her head. She was surprised to find that her sister-in-law was not there. She was not having a conversation with her sister-in-law at all—it was only a memory.

"Yes, that man is no good," she said again, and sighed. "I am not guilty of anything."

"Don't look over there!" she said to herself after a moment.

But it seemed to her that the hoodlum's eyes looked at her and smiled, from a corner somewhere.

Suddenly, an upsetting idea startled her: Compared to that hoodlum's wife in the home and the mistresses he kept outside, she was nothing. If the hoodlum missed out on seeing her today, it would be nothing to him. She had no power to injure him; she was not at all unique.

She abruptly stood up, and began to ask herself: "Is he just trifling with me?"

She picked up the blouse and sewing materials from their place atop the chest, "What do I care about that hoodlum?" she said. Why should she be afraid for that hoodlum to see her? Why should she be ashamed? She went out of that room and, as soon as she reached her own room, she felt as if her heart would stop. All the window shutters were wide open. She went around and quickly closed them all, but when she sat down to sew her blouse, she found it was too dark to work. She sat a few moments in silence. She would have to open a window, even if only a bit; she would open it so that nothing could be seen from over there, but just enough to let in a little light. She got up, slowly went toward the opening of the window and peered out. It seemed to her that there were two or three people in the room opposite. As she was trying to open the window shutters, she again felt as if her heart would stop. She turned around without opening the shutters, and went to the mirror to look at herself in the dim light. Her eyes looked as if she were sleeping, as did her whole countenance. She wanted to wake up that sleeping face. She smiled a little, and the smile spread across her entire face. She pressed her face against the mirror. She wanted to say, "Who says you're a beggar?"

But she turned away from the mirror abruptly.

"You are a beggar, and his wife is a queen! That hoodlum's wife is a queen, and you are a beggar!" it seemed someone said to her.

She felt certain that the hoodlum would think like that. When she turned toward the mirror again, she saw that her eyes had become very weary. Her whole face had completely withered up.

"How thin I've become!" she said.

She slowly opened the window.

"What am I but a beggar!" she said, opening another window.

"What do I care? They were just looking at me!"

Some dust had fallen from the beam onto the bedding. She shook it off.

"If someone wants to look at me, let him look! Why should I be shy?"

She wiped clean all the photos in the room.

"Men are like that: whenever they see some woman, they look at her as if they'd gobble her up!"

She made a vow that from now on she would not care about such things. Just as she had looked at him, from now on when she walked down the street she would look at other men. She had committed no more sin than that.

She sat in a corner at some distance from the window to sew her blouse. She didn't notice when five o'clock came and went, or when the sun left her room. Her mother called her to come and eat some *chiura*. She would have liked to make an excuse that she had a headache and refuse to eat, but instead she said, "I'll come in a minute." She looked at the room opposite without emotion. It was dark and empty. She hadn't noticed when they had gone. Drawing a long breath, she put the blouse away, left the room, and went upstairs. Her whole body was tired, and her head felt heavy. She heaved a great sigh that soothed her whole body. With that sigh, someone was saying to her, "Your husband is everything."

"He is my god," she said to herself.

That night, she fell asleep quickly and slept soundly.

Chapter Two

MISRI'S window shutters were wide open from early morning. After eating her rice, Misri sat in her room doing various tasks, but she felt no trace of interest or enthusiasm for anything. When she looked at herself in the mirror, she felt ugly; she hadn't put on any face cream or powder. On that day her heart was filled with emptiness, and her hands automatically set to work finishing sewing up her blouse. She took some of the clothes out of the chest and began to examine them. She felt like crying when she saw that insects had eaten part of a very expensive woolen shawl. She took it upstairs to air out in the sun. After she had folded all the clothes and put them back in the chest, she drew a long breath, and lay down.

She was thinking about what clothes she would take when she returned to her husband's house. She would take ordinary, unpretentious clothes to wear, but would not take anything fashionable. She did housework; she had no reason to go out. If she had to go out she would just make do with the simple house clothes she had.

She sighed again and said, "Now it will be a long time before I leave there! I won't come back here, and even if I do, I'll just stay here a day and then go back."

She thought about how there was nobody in her house, only her poor mother-in-law, who was old. Under no circumstances would Misri leave her house.

"Still, you should take something nice, for when people see you," it seemed that someone was telling her.

She began to fret, and she said to herself: "I am a beggar. I have stopped wearing nice clothes. I am ugly, ugly!"

She closed her eyes and lay down. Her mother came in and said, "How many times have I told you not to sleep in the daytime! Now you always have headaches. Headaches! In your parents' house you should also take care..."

Misri broke in angrily, in a teary voice. "If I just sit quietly for a moment, everyone says I have a headache! No matter what I do, everyone starts talking! No matter how much I try to make everyone happy, no one is satisfied. It would be better if I were dead!"

Her mother, dumbfounded, looked at her. After a bit, she said, "What did I say to you? All I said was you shouldn't sleep at the wrong time. Did I say anything to make you angry?"

Misri closed her eyes and pretended to sleep. She would sleep! If her head ached, let it ache! If she got a fever, let it come! Even if she died, so what!

Her mother said, "Do whatever you like. It's my duty to say something to you."

Her mother left. Her mother's affectionate anger began to soothe her body, and she began to fall into the boundless depths of her mind. She was falling asleep. At that moment, it seemed to her that something was being said, a voice calling to someone, piercing her eardrums, and she abruptly awoke and sat up: in the street outside that hoodlum was calling out, "Ramman! Ramman!" Misri, hardly awake, reached a window. That hoodlum was standing in the street. Now he was looking up at Misri from below. His eyes registered surprise for only a moment, and after that the eyes smiled and he appeared to be saying something to her. She could not remain in the window, and went away. She also, unwittingly, was smiling and the, astonished at her own smile. She sat down on the trunk and remained sitting there.

She could not gather the courage to go near the window again, nor did she have the power to leave the room. She did not have the nerve to move. She was afraid of those eyes that looked as if they wanted to speak, those eyes that smiled when they saw her. She was completely unable to move.

Her mother called, "Misri! Misri!" from above. Misri didn't answer. Misri didn't want anyone to hear the slightest sound from her.

Her sister-in-law came in and said, "Your mother has been calling you for a long time. I thought maybe you were sleeping."

"Why was she calling me?" Misri was smiling as she spoke to her sister-in-law. Her sister-in-law looked around, looked at herself. "Is something wrong?"

"No, nothing! Go ahead, sister-in-law. I'm coming, just as soon as I do something."

"It doesn't look as if you're doing anything."

"There is something." Misri looked smilingly toward the window, and said, "You go. I'll come in a minute."

Her sister-in-law looked at her suspiciously, and then looked toward the window. When she started to walk toward the window, Misri cried out, "Oh! Don't go there—there's a ghost!"

"Let's have a look," said her sister-in-law, continuing to the window.

Misri also got up suddenly, feeling very afraid. "It's nothing. Just that hoodlum over there."

"What?" Her sister-in-law stopped and tried to read Misri's face. "Look!" said Misri in a complaining voice, and went toward the window.

Across the way, that hoodlum was standing in the window, together with Ramman. The hoodlum was looking at Misri with those smiling eyes. Ramman, pretending not to see Misri, had twisted his head around to look down the street. Now the hoodlum's eyes were shining. Those eyes signaled her, unmistakably signaled her. Misri fell away from the window as if she had received an electrical shock, and with the speed of lightning, she left the room. Her sister-in-law, who had for some time been standing dumbfounded, slowly followed.

Some time later, Misri again entered the room. Now she was carrying her baby niece. Looking around the room, she felt as if the room were not real. Her niece pulled on a lock of her hair. Misri started, as if the baby had just now suddenly come in contact with her body, and she had been carrying her niece without realizing what she was doing. Those eyes were dancing as they glanced here and there; those eyes were giving a signal. Misri felt that she had to get some things from her room quickly, and rushed to and fro about the room. She stopped at the photo of her grandmother. It seemed that her grandmother was staring at her with concern. She turned away and opened a drawer. In the drawer there were bottles and other things all mixed together. She turned around and approached the mirror. Her dancing eyes appeared in the mirror, very much as if giving a sign. The baby she was carrying cried a little, and Misri began to swing her gently around the room. As she was swinging the child about, Misri reached the window and pointed out the cat running on the roof of the house opposite. The baby again pulled on Misri's hair. Then Misri remained there by the window, and gave the baby a kiss on the cheek.

In the window opposite, that hoodlum was standing, alone. Misri lowered her eyes and gently said to the baby, "Tell him not to look at me like that."

That hoodlum's hand was raised a little. Misri pretended not to notice and looked beyond. That hand moved and made the shape of something; it moved. Misri, shocked, watched that hand. That hand was calling to her shamelessly. She raised her eyes and looked at the hoodlum's face. "What nerve!" Nonetheless, that hoodlum's whole body was smiling.

After a moment, Misri felt nervous and looked up and down the street, but there was no one she knew who would have seen that man's gesture. However, it seemed to her that someone might have seen them, and she felt breathless with fear; hastily she closed the window with a bang.

Evening came, then night. Now that hoodlum wasn't in the house opposite. She opened the window of her own room. Now that the hand wasn't there, she could open the window without worry. The street had become quiet, and there was still some time before the midnight cannon would sound. A lamp was still burning in that room of the house opposite. It was getting cold in her room, and Misri sat shivering. She was not wearing a shawl. It was very quiet, everything was very quiet. Her mind also was very quiet, and she was terrified.

"Sister-in-law knows!" she said to herself.

"What fault do I have? If he called to me, what have I done? Did I go?" she answered her own query.

But she had an impression that the hoodlum was in a corner of that room gesturing to her, and she was ready to go. In confusion she pressed both hands against her head. Now she was awake and looked around. "What must that hoodlum think I am?" she said to herself.

Her sister-in-law had finished the housework and was probably washing the dishes. Misri slowly closed the window and put on a shawl. Then she picked up the brass pitcher and looked inside. There was some water left. She could only go to her sister-in-law under the pretext of getting some water. She poured the water into the chamber pot and went into the kitchen with the pitcher.

Her sister-in-law was sitting on the verandah scrubbing the pots. Misri said, "I came to get some water."

Her sister-in-law did not answer. It seemed to her that her sister-in-law said, "You didn't come here to get water."

"Some dust fell into the water I got just a while ago," Misri spoke again.

As she dipped water from the pot, she said, "Sister-in-law!"

Her sister-in-law looked at her. She didn't look at her sister-in-law, but tried to smile. "Sister-in-law, these men!"

Misri felt that her sister-in-law was looking at her. She said, "These men! Such characters! It's a great joke to make them dance around!"

She tried to bring a smile to her face, but couldn't. Nevertheless, she continued. "They think they own all the women they see! All men think themselves kings. It's fun to make them play, fool them..."

She was almost shouting, then laughed, then suddenly stopped laughing. She was startled by her own laugh that didn't ring true. Sister-in-law stopped cleaning the pots and looked at her.

She again stopped and was silent. Sister-in-law did not laugh, and after a moment said, "Women are a helpless lot."

Misri glanced at her sister-in-law. "Helpless?"

"If a man's eyes look at you, you're impure, just like that!" Sister-in-law said. "And who can stop the mouths of people who talk?"

Misri hadn't realized that her sister-in-law had such thoughtful opinions. She looked at her sister-in-law's face for a moment and said, "What are you saying, sister-in-law? Just because we women are helpless, can a man say whatever he likes?"

Her sister-in-law did not answer. Misri looked at her as if it were her sister-in-law who had criticized her. After a moment, Misri said, "Can't I rip off the face of anyone who criticizes me?"

Now her sister-in-law looked at her. It seemed to Misri that she was saying, "You couldn't rip off anything."

"Why couldn't I?" Misri said.

The kitchen became quiet. There was no sound except for the sound of her sister-in-law scrubbing pots. Misri took the filled pitcher and said, "What can I do? That man is looking at me from the house opposite. I can't go close those eyes. I can't keep the windows of my room closed all day, either."

Her sister-in-law still said nothing, and continued to scrub the pots. Misri spoke again. "When one's own mind is pure..."

She again looked immediately towards her sister-in-law, but her sister-in-law did not want to talk with her. It seemed that her sister-in-law did not believe what Misri said, and that she had fallen in her sister-in-law's eyes. Misri said angrily, "I am not afraid of anyone! I am not a child. I'm not afraid of you!"

She turned around abruptly, picked up the pitcher, and went downstairs.

The next morning, when Misri awoke from sleep, she opened her eyes, surprised. While she slept, she had forgotten all of yesterday's happenings. In her sleep that man was not himself. She got up and went upstairs to the kitchen. Her sister-in-law, the same as every day, was turned towards the hearth, working. Recalling her talk with her sister-ion-law the night before, she felt deeply ashamed. She could not see her sister-in-law's face. It was as if she had been defeated and her sister-in-law had won. It seemed to Misri that if she left the kitchen, her defeat would be compounded. She sat down to cut the vegetables, but her sister-in-law did not turn around to look, and she was throwing some husks onto the fire. The sparkling cheap designs of her sari were stretched taut on part of her back. It seemed to her that pride had expanded her sister-in-law's body. When she saw her sister-in-law's body, she felt envious. She didn't want to look helpless and she certainly did not want to appear weak in front of her sister-in-law. Various words began to form in her mouth. She began to search for words that would hurt her sister-in-law, but she couldn't think of anything.

She said gently, "Is this all the potatoes we have?"

"No one went to the shop today," said sister-in-law, who was turned toward the hearth. "We'll have to substitute with a few more onions."

The kitchen became silent again, and the sound of water boiling gradually increased. After a moment, Misri said, "I came here to my mother's house to get a rest. I don't get a moment to myself here either. There is work all the time, one thing after another!"

She wanted to say something serious, but she felt tangled up and fell silent, and her sister-in-law had still not turned to look at her. But the water boiled over, and the kitchen was filled with the sound of the fire sputtering.

"Why should I be afraid of anyone?" Misri said.

Her sister-in-law still did not turn around to look. Misri was boiling, but collected herself to say, "Sister-in-law, why are you sitting like that today?"

Her sister-in-law turned to look at her and said, "Why? What have I done?"

"I won't stand to be insulted by anyone!"

"What did I say? What did I do wrong?" Sister-in-law said, frightened.

"In you mind, do you think I'm a whore?"

Sister-in-law's face changed color. She started to scream, but the scream stopped in her throat. She said breathlessly, "I didn't say that!"

At that moment they heard the sound of Misri's mother coming up the stairs. The kitchen again became silent, and it seemed that the intense talk in the kitchen was cautiously suspended. Her mother came in and said, "Has the water boiled?"

Sister-in-law shook her head to indicate it had.

Misri suddenly cried in a tearful voice, "Mother, don't we have any honor?"

Her mother, not comprehending, looked at her in surprise.

"Don't we have any *dharma*? Don't we have a respectable family? Why is it that Ramman in the house opposite, whoever he finds he brings there..."

Her mother continued to look at her in astonishment.

"Does that hoodlum, that gangster, have the right to keep watching us? He is watching us! We..."

With these words, Misri left the kitchen.

She could not face her sister-in-law, nor could she look her mother in the eye. She was alone, and confused.

In the afternoon, her father had gone out, and Misri was just leaving his room after doing some chores there when a small girl from the neighborhood stood in front of her. The girl held out her hand and said, "Here—this is for you."

"What?" Misri was surprised and held out her hand.

As she placed a piece of paper in Misri's hand, the girl said, "A letter, from that man who comes to Ramman's over there. He said not to give it to anyone but you."

The color left Misri's face and she was overcome by fear. She looked at the girl speechlessly. The girl, taking fright, said, "He told me to give it to you, so I... brought it..."

The girl confusedly ran down the stairs.

Misri held out the letter to return it, but the girl had already reached the ground floor. She tried to call to the girl, but the words trembled for a moment in her throat and disappeared. Then she crumpled up the letter and hid it in her fist.

She tried to throw it away, but she couldn't find a place to throw it. She tried to read it, but found no place to sit and read. There was no one in her father's room, so she went in, but it seemed that someone was there, so she came out again. She thought of going into her own room, but thinking she might be seen from that other house, she came back. She looked in the kitchen, but her sister-in-law was there doing something. The letter was moving about inside her fist, as if it wanted to drop from her hand. She tightened her fist. She started, and jumped up to go to the roof, where the small *puja* room was located. She went into the *puja* room, disturbing a flock of sparrows eating the bits of sacred rice offerings left from the *puja*; they flew out the window in a flurry of wings. She started, then looked about her. Images of Mahadev and Parvati, Shesh-shayi Vishnu, Radhakrishna, the Astamatrika, Taleju, and Betal-Bhairav were arranged on the wall. Misri looked for a moment at the picture of Bhagwan seated on a lion throne; the image was placed atop a sacred stone. Then, looking at a *shaligram*, she tried to remember something. At Pashupati Temple, an Astabakra yogi who always sat on the ground wrapped up in a cloth, cried out "Holy *shaligrams* from the Ganges!"

From somewhere this whole line of thought was interrupted. It seemed that the letter in her hand was moving about, trying to escape. Suddenly it seemed all the gods and goddesses were assaulting her, so she went out.

"I'm going to throw this letter away!" she said. But having reached the edge of the roof, she recoiled; someone was sitting on the roof of the house opposite. She turned back, and it seemed the letter was frightened of being held in her hand. She slowly went downstairs, opened the door of the storeroom, and went inside. Large pots and baskets were scattered here and there, like lifeless creatures, all crowded together. It seemed to her that they would all watch her read the letter. She just stood there, then, smiling a little she pulled herself together and leaned against a large pot. If her mother came in to see, she would show her the letter and say, "Look! That character sent me a letter!" What did she have to be afraid of? What had she done?-- she thought.

She slowly opened her fist. The crumpled letter fell on the floor. She spread open the letter and read: "I love you. I have never loved anyone like this before. Do you love me or not? Send your reply."

The letters got entangled with one another and began to dance. She read it again, and again. Then the letters ceased dancing, and remained staring at her.

"I love you. Do you love me or not? Send your reply." She repeated it again and again in her mind. The letter fell to the floor; it stared up at her, waiting for her reply.

"I am married! Whether I love you or not—what difference does it make?" she said to herself.

There was a sound as if someone might be climbing the stairs. The cat jumped in through a small window. She nervously picked up the letter and tore it to pieces. Then it was quiet again. The pieces of the torn-up letter were in her hand.

It was extremely quiet. Up until a few moments ago, it had seemed that those large pots were speaking, but now they were silent. Just as if she had been working hard for a long time, she felt very tired and closed her eyes. She had a feeling that she was being violently pulled toward her husband's house. She felt this impression for a long time. But then another image came to mind: she was in the arms of that hoodlum, and his lips were quite close to hers.

Misri started breathlessly. The pieces of the letter had fallen from her hand and were scattered on the floor.

She tried to get up, but couldn't. Tiredness was soothing her entire body, and she closed her eyes again.

After a moment, she saw another image: that hoodlum was pulling her along behind, through narrow lane after narrow lane. And suddenly that hoodlum no longer looked like the "hoodlum"—he had the face of her husband!

She started again. A breeze was scattering the bits of torn letter and turning them over. One piece was dancing right in front of her. On that piece, there were only two letters: "lo..."

Misri suddenly became frightened, as if she had just realized that she was in grave danger. She picked up the scattered pieces of the letter and put them inside her blouse. She said, "I have to burn these."

After a while Misri was alone in the kitchen, and with unblinking eyes she watched the pieces of the letter burn in the clay stove-pot. The pieces burned completely, and stopped smoking. When the paper was completely reduced to ashes, she went to the kitchen window and sat down.

It seemed to her that she was completely alone. She had no one; she was completely alone. Her mother, father, brother, and sister-in-law were all far away. Feeling completely desolate, she sat alone by the window. It seemed to her that her husband was watching her from somewhere. She had an impression of being in an enclosure, and her husband was peering at her from beyond that enclosure. Those eyes were solitary, just as Misri's were.

It was as if she were saying to her husband, "I burned the letter. Now, that hoodlum won't look at me!"

She got up and went into her mother's room. Her mother wasn't there, and she felt extremely relieved. She hoped on one would see her, as she wanted to be alone. She sat in that room alone.

But after a bit, her mother came into the room. Misri turned her face to the wall.

Her mother said, "What's wrong?"

Misri gathered her courage, looked at her mother and said, "Today they'll come to take me home, right?"

Her mother was surprised. "You sent word to them that you would come two days later, Monday."

"I really must go today. Here, I..."

Her mother came close to her and said, "What's the matter with you? Nowadays I see... Now, why are you crying?"

Misri sobbed quietly. Her mother said, "Why are you crying? If you don't want to go, stay three or four days longer."

She cried more, and her mother's eyes began to glisten with tears of sympathy.

At last Misri's sobbing stopped, and she pierced the curtain of tears to look at her mother. No, mother doesn't know anything.

After her mother left the room and Misri was alone again, she thought, "Not two days from now—how would it be if they called for me today?" From now on she would stay at her mother's house only for a day. She took an oath mentally.

It was night. After eating her rice, Misri went downstairs. When she reached the level of her bedroom, she became speechless with astonishment. Mute, she looked steadily for a moment at the young servant girl from her husband's house.

The girl said, "They say to come today. Your mother-in-law has become ill and can't do anything. The master said, 'Bring her back for sure.'"

Only the words, "All right" fell from Misri's lips.

"This morning, the master cooked his own rice. His niece had gone home for a *puja.* If I were only old enough to do the cooking..."

Suddenly Misri wanted to hold and girl and cry. When her mother came from upstairs Misri regained her composure. Her mother said, "Misri is not well. Didn't we say two days later?"

The girl said, "Yes, two days later. But what can we do? Niece left yesterday, and now the master's mother is ill. Oh, what a cough! She can't eat or sleep. When she starts coughing, she can't stop."

"This morning, the master cooked his own rice!" said the girl, smiling.

Her mother said to Misri, "You did say you would go today."

Misri looked at her mother for a moment with pity. No, her mother knew nothing. And, seeing her mother's manner, she said "Yes!" angrily.

She wheeled around brusquely and went into her room. She hurriedly put on her clothes.

Her mother said, "In fifteen days we will have *Shraddha,* the yearly mourning ceremony."

Misri opened the chest and roughly pulled out some other clothes.

Her mother said, "Come really early in the morning on that day."

Misri put some clothes in a bundle.

Her mother said, "Whatever you do, don't eat sour or spicy food, as I've told you."

Misri's anger faded and in her throat she felt tears rising. She gave the traditional respectful bow to her mother, in preparation for departure.

Her mother said, "Aren't you going to take this blouse?"

Misri shook her head no in response.

It was difficult to stop her tears. She went into her father's room to bow respectfully, and returned immediately.

Her father asked from inside the room, "When will you come back again?"

Her mother said abruptly, "She's coming for the *Shraddha* ceremony."

Her sister-in-law hesitantly came in and said, "When will you be coming again? At *Shraddha*? Please come! You see I'm alone here to do everything. Come a day early!"

Now Misri was able to see her sister-in-law's face. Her eyes were humble, and Misri wanted to say something, but she forgot what it was.

Her older brother would come to the house only after the cannon sounded, and her younger brother had gone to study. She felt that she was going away for many days, for always, and she had to see the faces of her two brothers once before she left. This made her pause for a moment, but the street was dark, and it was already late. She had to go very far, very far! So she would not get to meet her brothers. She slowly descended the stairs.

Outside the door of the house, she found herself in front of the house opposite, and it seemed as if the house were blocking the street. She moved quickly to get beyond that house. When she got well beyond, she remembered the window of that room in the house opposite. That window had been closed. It seemed to her that someone was following her. In the street an old man was coughing as he walked behind her. In front of her, a group of men were standing around at a tobacco shop. Her heart began to beat fast; maybe the hoodlum was in that group. Her gait slowed down. The group became very quiet and began to look at her. She shrank back as she passed them; that hoodlum was not there.

"After tomorrow, he won't be able to see me!" she said to herself.

A little further on, she said, "He will be disappointed. What a joke!"

Chapter Three

MISRI arrived in front of her husband's house in a narrow lane near Indrachowk, and came to a dead stop. It seemed to her that she had suddenly arrived there in one instant, from a place very far away. Inside, to climb the stairs from the ground floor, you have to go around the staircase from the other side; she forgot to turn and nearly ran into the wall, as if she were a stranger coming here for the first time.

As she was climbing the stairs, she heard her mother-in-law's hoarse voice, a voice punctuated with coughs. "Seti, Seti! Has my daughter-in-law come back yet?"

That voice overwhelmed her. Seti, the servant girl, said, "She's come!"

The house became silent, as if sunk in fathomless sorrow. Misri felt like sitting down right there, crouching on the stairs. Her husband's room was on the upper floor near the stairs. That room's door was open and the light from the lamp inside fell on the corridor. Misri knew that her husband was in the room, but he did not come to the door to see her. It seemed to Misri that he, too, did not feel much enthusiasm. She went upstairs to greet her mother-in-law.

Her mother-in-law looked exhausted. She had grown thinner, and her cheeks were more sunken. Her eyes had shrunk to two black eyeballs shining from two dark pits. Those two eyes searched Misri from top to bottom. Those two eyes briefly examined Misri's clothes and appearance. Misri gave her mother-in-law a formal greeting by touching her forehead to her mother-in-law's foot, and she felt the coldness of that foot move to her forehead. When Misri raised her head to look at her mother-in-law, she saw envy dancing in her mother-in-law's eyes.

After a moment, her mother-in-law drew a long sigh and said, "You must understand what has happened in the house. I have become disabled. There is no one here who's even capable of heating water. Only poor Seti—and what can she do?"

Misri gazed for a moment at her mother-in-law's hollow eyes, her hollow cheeks, her thin body. Misri felt a cruel laugh coloring her face, trying to force its way out. She struggled to make her face look concerned, but that laugh was still lurking about, and she stopped that laugh from escaping by turning her face aside.

Her husband still showed no eagerness, no interest. He still hadn't come out of his room. Misri was filled with the same derisive laugh for her husband. She reached his door, stopped suddenly and examined herself cursorily. She suddenly felt like a wilted flower that had just fallen to the ground. And then she laughed that same cruel laugh at herself.

She stood fidgeting at the door for a moment. Her husband had not yet called her. She no longer felt the shyness, the fear of going into her new husband's room she had as a newly-wed; she now felt detached from those feelings. She sighed. Now she just felt a sense of the inferiority of everything, including herself.

She went into the room. Her husband's dispassionate eyes smiled a little as he remained silent. She set her bundle of clothing on the big wooden chest that had been given as part of her dowry. The wooden chest had become soiled, and had lost its color. Her husband still said nothing. She thought of how her older brother, when her sister-in-law came back from her own mother's house, would sort through the clothes and things in her bag and ask, "Is this something new?" Her husband did not speak.

Suddenly her husband spoke. "The day before yesterday you said you had a headache. You still look a little ill."

Misri felt the sarcastic smile reach her face as she faced her husband—how naive he was! He had believed the falsehood that she had sent back with Seti from her parents' house.

She said, "Could I have come back if I were sick?"

"No, why should you come back if you were sick? You wouldn't get any rest here!"

Now, Misri began to feel as if she were actually ill. She gently sat down. Actually, she would have been relieved had she really been ill.

"That was just a lie I told the day before yesterday," she said.

Her husband looked as though he didn't believe her, and she gave him a look filled with kindness.

"Don't you believe me?" she asked.

Her husband said nothing, did not so much as say the word "lie." She sat waiting. He did not rush to embrace Misri. If only he had become angry and they had quarreled—even if he had cursed her, Misri would have felt relieved.

The lane was quiet. The cannon had fired, and the lights in the room had been put out. Misri did not sleep next to her husband; she slept in separate bedding. Her husband had not believed that she was quite well yet. Misri was not sleepy. She was enveloped by darkness, and the darkness caused her to see all kinds of shapes. Across the room her husband was sleeping, and she heard his breathing; he was in deep slumber. Misri tossed and turned restlessly. It would have been better had she awoken gravely ill; even if her husband had used her body cruelly, she would have felt better.

In the early morning, her husband woke up before she did, and went downstairs to the toilet. Her husband's shape was still formed by the quilt under which he had been sleeping. Misri looked at that form for some time. The sight of that hollowed-out shape in the bedding made her feel depressed; she felt a deep desolation.

She got hot water and brought it in to her mother-in-law's room. She looked at her mother-in-law's thin wasted form for some time, and she placed the stove-pot on the ground. Watching her mother-in-law take the medicine, she again felt desolate. She felt that desolation about her mother-in-law and about herself. She looked at her mother-in-law through a layer of tears in her eyes. After a moment, she saw that her mother-in-law's eyes were just like those of her husband. Her mother-in-law's appearance and that of her husband were quite similar, and their noses curved in the same way.

"Isn't it time to make the rice?" her mother-in-law asked.

"Yes!" Misri put the medicine bag away in the round cane basket, and put the small clay stove in a corner.

"Feed him well!"

Misri gazed at her mother-in-law's face. Her mother-in-law, examining her own hands as she turned them over, said, "He is a very simple man.

When he was very young his father died. I had so much trouble raising him—so much trouble! Now, how many days do I have left?"

Misri could say nothing, and hastily left the room.

Later, Misri was cooking the meal. Her husband came out of the *puja* room, which was behind a wooden partition in the kitchen. When she saw the devotion in his face, Misri again felt emptiness in her heart. She had the impression that those eyes full of religious devotion showed illness, helplessness, and the silent neediness of an orphan.

Her husband sat down to eat his morning meal and she gave him a little more of the vegetables and scooped out more rice than usual. Her husband said, "Why so much? Why did you add ghee? I've got a cold."

Misri said irritably, "You always have a cold. Don't be afraid—eat! Nothing will happen!"

As her husband continued to eat, she said, "I don't think there's enough salt on the vegetables. You look as if it tastes bad. I've forgotten how to cook; I've lost the knack."

"What? There's enough salt," said her husband, surprised.

"I don't think it tastes good," she said, to test him.

"It is good. Who said it wasn't?"

Misri felt surprised. If he had said there was not enough salt, or that the food didn't taste good, it would have been fun. "How simple-minded he is. He is not able to joke," she thought.

After her husband had washed his hands, rinsed his mouth, and gone downstairs, she was surprised that she had forgotten to give him the customary formal salutation. She went downstairs to do so, thinking that he was probably awaiting her obeisance. Her husband's feet, which she had to touch in formal greeting, were thin and brittle. After giving the salutation, it occurred to her that her husband did not jokingly withdraw his feet to prevent her from giving the obeisance, as her brother did to her sister-in-law to tease her, nor did he knowingly neglect to allow her obeisance, which would keep her from eating all day, as a good wife would not eat her own meal without performing that formality.

After her husband disappeared down the stairs on his way to the office, it seemed that someone else was breathing within her breast, and she sat pondering for a long time.

After everyone had finished eating, Misri was applying a layer of clay to the hearth, and Seti was scouring the pots on the small terrace. Misri said, "Seti, what would you do if your husband grabbed you by the hair and dragged you down the street?"

Seti, absorbed in scouring the pots, was surprised by this question addressed by her mistress, and looked at her a moment before answering. "If he were to drag me along like that, couldn't I shame him right in the street? Is he any better than I am?"

"Why don't you go back to your husband?"

"Why should I go to him if he can't feed me?"

"If your husband is unable to feed you, should you leave him?"

Before Seti could answer, Misri, as if asking herself, gently said, "Isn't it a sin?"

Seti then looked surprised for a moment, peered at Misri's face and said, "It depends on one's own caste. In our caste, it's not a sin."

"It's not a sin, even if you run off with another man?" Misri asked in the same voice as before.

"I'd sign a divorce paper."

Misri looked at Seti's face curiously. Seti said, "That one! The fool couldn't afford to feed me—in fact, he beat me! He didn't give me a single day of peace. Even during the day, after he drank rice beer, he just started beating me."

"Why would he beat you?" She spoke in a sad voice, as if she were awaiting her own beating.

"Who knows? He'd just start beating me. He wasn't able to provide food for me—but I would have stayed with him even with a half-empty stomach." Uncertain for a moment, she looked at Misri and, in a voice eager to reveal her story, said, "He was suspicious of me, for no reason! He said I was making eyes at Chamcha, a boy in the neighborhood. He suspected that I was having an affair."

"Suspected?" Misri asked, intrigued.

"Yes!" Seti laughed and said, "Suspected for no reason! I told him a thousand times that it wasn't true. When he was sober he believed me, and admitted he couldn't provide for me, and sometimes cried. The next day he would drink rice beer again and the same thing would happen. It's amazing to me how he would be suspicious like that."

"And he beat you! How did he beat you?' Misri said with a sigh, as if she herself had received the beatings. "With his hand?" she asked, in a strangled voice.

Seti, not understanding Misri for a moment, was surprised. "With whatever he cold find—not just his hand!"

Misri felt gooseflesh for some time. "How cold he beat her?" she said in her mind. She imagined Seti's husband beating Seti. She tried to feel hatred for the husband and sympathy for Seti, but she could not muster any hatred for the husband, and in fact felt a kind of envy for Seti.

During the day, Misri was doing some errands in her mother-in-law's room, and her mother-in-law watched her work without speaking. After some time, she said, "Did Haribhakta eat well before he left?"

"He ate."

The events of the past were taking shape in her mother-in-law's eyes. There were so many ups and downs in those events. As Misri began to mend a sheet, her mother-in-law said, "I was a helpless widow! When the boy was small, his father passed on. I wasn't able to feed him well, and he didn't get good food like my brother-in-law's kids. I was hiding him in my room."

After a moment, Misri felt her mother-in-law looking at her intently. She slowly raised her eyes to look at her mother-in-law. It seemed to her that her mother-in-law's eyes were filled with envy. Those eyes seemed to say, "I have to hand over this son I raised to *her*, to this woman who came from who knows where."

She felt some satisfaction at her mother-in-law's envy. The envy enhanced her husband's character.

Her mother-in-law began again to speak of past events, of which Misri had often heard before. She could picture these events, and having heard them so often had almost become a part of these memories.

Her mother-in-law had become a widow when she was very young, and Misri's husband Haribhakta had become fatherless. Her mother-in-law had great difficulty in protecting her virtue. Wherever she turned it seemed that people were talking, but the sight of her son's face made her ready to endure all hardship. As Haribhakta had no father, it fell upon his father's elder brother to take care of the two of them. They had little inheritance, and the two of them, mother and son, were an added burden to the household. Her brother-in-law's wife suspected they had come to rob her of her own portion. Misri's mother-in-law was surprised that even the children of those who were earning were aware of their parents' difficulties. Mother and son were subjected to contempt and insults from everyone, and were the object of many piercing words. They had to endure so many difficulties as Haribhakta grew up and she grew old. Haribhakta finally achieved the fourth level of the civil service examination, and his uncle, by asking around, found him work; after seven years the boy rose to the rank of supervisor. Misri's mother-in-law wanted so much to die during that time. Should she hold her son tightly and jump into a well? Or should the two of them drink poison and die? She harped on this refrain over and over. But when Haribhakta called to her, and quarreled with her, or laughed with her, the torment disappeared without a trace, and Misri's mother-in-law then relented. She thought, "I have sinned in my past lives. This is written in my karma. This poor Haribhakta has done no wrong, committed no transgression. The fault is all mine!" For this reason, she would not leave her son, and would not go off and die alone. Haribhakta had been aware of all this misery since childhood. For this reason, if anyone swore at him, he would walk off hesitatingly, would speak fearfully. He was subject to contempt whether in the house or outside, and became afraid of everyone. He could not speak well. He became timid. His mother was the only person he was not afraid of. When he was a child, there was little to nourish him, and even though he ate only rice, it was always as if he were eating poison. For that reason, he was weak and helpless.

Her mother-in-law, sometimes speaking softly, sometimes loudly, sometimes in a sighing voice, sometimes quickly or gently, painted a picture of the sorrows and joys of mother and son that danced before Misri's eyes.

Her mother-in-law was silent for a short time, then spoke again. "If I hadn't been there, how much more misery would Haribhakta have experienced? Realizing that is what has kept me alive up to now."

Her mother-in-law stopped talking, and a deep silence fell. Misri finished sewing on the sheet, and looked around for some other work to do.

"Well, after I die!" Her mother-in-law spoke after a long sigh. Glancing at Misri for a moment, she spoke again. "I can die after I see the face of my grandson."

Misri felt something like a jolt, then dismay. She turned her face to the wall and stared, astonished. After a moment, she quickly gathered up the small stove and went upstairs to bring some fire.

She had been married for three years, and there was still no child in her womb. She shook her head. Yes, perhaps that was the reason her mind was suffocating: was her womb awaiting a baby, a fine baby? She was upset like this because she hadn't become pregnant. It seemed to her that a baby would rescue her from this unknown terror. And the desire for the baby would swell up to include love and affection for her husband.

Her mother had said one day, "Misri has just turned 20. She'll have a baby when the time is right. Why should she put up with all that trouble at such a young age?"

With the mention of a baby, Misri had turned her head away in disgust. Now her whole body was carried away with "A baby!" She put the clay stove on the floor and sat down, lost in thought. She imagined what the face of her baby would be like. Then she roughly set the image aside, hurriedly lit a fire in the stove and blew on it—the baby's face had become the face of that man in the house opposite! She blew forcefully on the fire in the stove. Nonetheless, that baby's face had become the face of the hoodlum.

She repeated again and again to herself: "No baby for me! Not for me!"

Her husband was tired when he returned from the office, and Misri put curried potatoes and *chiura* before him. She watched him as he ate. The veins in her husband's throat trembled, and his Adam's apple moved up and down. It seemed to Misri that he was killing the enjoyment that came with eating. His thin helpless body remained stuck in the circumstances of terrible suffering in his past. Misri's eyes filled with tears of pity and compassion. She wanted to speak, but no words came forth. Her husband looked so tired that he, too, could not bring himself to speak. He just looked at Misri with gratitude, and showed a spark of happiness at receiving love. Misri turned her face away.

After he finished eating, her husband picked up the small clay stove, filled the hookah pipe with tobacco and started to go downstairs, when suddenly Misri felt the unkind laugh filling her body. She asked herself angrily, "Why didn't he ask me to put the tobacco in for him? What is he afraid of?" But then she restrained herself and said, jokingly, "So you're smoking a hookah, like an old man?"

Her husband was surprised for a moment, then looked at her and said, "Hookah tobacco tastes better than cigarettes, and it's cheaper, too."

To Misri, it was as if her own words were giving her a slap. If it was cheap, then there was nothing more to say.

When Misri came into their room at night, her husband asked, "You don't have a headache or anything, do you?"

Misri laughed that same unkind laugh, and again said angrily, "No, why should it worry you? Who said I was sick?"

Her husband was surprised and said a little fearfully, "I was just asking."

Misri swallowed the unkind laugh with a gulp and remained quiet. If her husband had become angry, she too would have been angry. They would have quarreled, and then she would have been calm! If he had not suddenly felt fearful, Misri would have been relieved.

Watching her husband's rhythmic smoking of the hookah for a moment, Misri said, "Why do you treat me like a child?"

She was surprised by her own words. Actually, that man seemed to her like a child, very child-like and helpless.

Misri took the pipe her husband was smoking and put it aside; she sat next to him, took his cheek in her hand and gave him a kiss.

Now his lips were close to Misri's lips. Misri said gently, "Don't you love me? Don't you care?"

Again she surprised herself with her words, and she turned her face away. "How false these words are!" she thought, and it seemed that his whole body let forth a sigh. "You have not loved me as much as you should, and you haven't taken care of me as much as you should have." She turned her head again and her lips found those of her husband.

The next afternoon, her mother-in-law was sleeping in her room. Seti had finished her work and had fetched two pots of water before she went out. A man came to collect the niece's clothes, and Misri sent the clothes away with him. She was watching at the window when she spotted a man's back and jumped back suddenly from the window. Then it seemed to her that she was seeing things, so she went back to look out the window. But she was startled again, and left the window. This time it was not the man's back. He was facing her, and it was that hoodlum. Their eyes met. His face, along with his whole body, was smiling, just as at first.

After a moment, when she was in her room folding her husband's clothes, she thought, "He came here by accident. Can't just anyone walk in the street?"

After she had folded the clothes and put them in the chest, she suddenly had the impression that that man was climbing the stairs. She cupped her ear to listen, but no, it was her mind playing tricks on her. After a moment, it seemed to her that he had entered the room. Fearfully, she looked about, but again it was an illusion. Then she put the door bar in place, closing up the room.

That night, Misri could not go into her own room for a long time. She stayed in her mother-in-law's room doing this and that, and at last, when her mother-in-law told her to sleep, she got up. When she reached her bedroom, she saw that her husband was not asleep. Confused, she stepped back. She wanted to forget the afternoon's incident and relax, but there was her husband, who hadn't yet gone to bed. After a moment, the same unkind laugh lingered on her lips, and she sat down.

To her husband's mundane conversation she answered only "yes" and "no." She didn't want anyone to speak with her; she wanted to sit very, very quietly. At the same time, she wanted to do something so extraordinary that she would not care even if she did not sleep all night, but she could not determine what it was.

For some time, the room was quiet. Suddenly Misri wanted to talk, and in a joking tone she said, "Do you just say you love me, or do you really mean it? How can a man's words be believed?"

"Why, do you have some doubts?" He tried to adopt a similar joking tone.

"Yes. Men are good at covering up," she said without smiling.

Her husband became serious. "Honestly, I've never looked at anyone else."

Misri lost all desire to joke. Seeing her husband's seriousness, she felt confused. In fact, if this man said that he had been seeing someone, she would have been content. If he had said he loved someone, or someone loved him, she would have been content. She wanted to scratch his eyes out, but they peered at her like those of a baby looking at his mother.

Afterwards, Misri felt a kind of aversion. Saying her head hurt, she turned over and slept, covering her face. Her husband, taking her at her word, stroked her head. She moved her husband's hand away and said, "Stop, you're keeping me from going to sleep."

The next day she did not go near the window facing the street. She bolted the window from inside.

Just as he did every day, her husband, after eating his *chiura,* brought some fire for the hookah. Irritably, she said, "Why should a man always stay at home every evening?"

Her husband, surprised, looked at her. "What can I do? I get tired working in the office all day."

"If you went outside for a walk, you wouldn't be so tired; your body would be healthy. My father and older brother never stay in the house, come what may."

"Where would I go? Where would I walk by myself?"

"Don't you have any friends to play cards with?" Misri held her anger in check.

"All my friends are different now. Some have been promoted, some—who knows! The people at the office aren't really friends. You tell me to play cards! If you get the habit of card-playing, gambling..."

"Gambling?" Misri looked at him sharply. Her ear heard the noise of playing cards and carom in the house next to her room in her parents' house. After some time, she said, "In that case, go offer your services to your boss. Every day after work, my uncle goes to wait at his boss's house."

Her husband now looked quite helpless. After a long time, he said, "Why should I go offer my services to someone, like in the Rana era? Now things have changed. And if I went to my boss's—who would notice your husband there? You have to be a secretary, a *subba*, a *sardar*. Your husband is not one to go curry favor under pretense of doing some office work."

Misri was silent, and forgot all that she wanted to say. Now that unkind laugh played on her lips.

The next morning she saw that hoodlum walking in the street. Only his back was visible and his form was like a line drawn on paper. That line was lost at a turn in the lane. He might come back again, and thinking that he might return, she moved away from the window. "He's started to come around in the morning, too," she said to herself.

She had no hope that he would come in the morning, but she could feel no surprise. Since he had come this morning, he wouldn't come again in the evening, she thought, and sat in the window. However, without realizing it she felt the suspense of waiting. In the meantime, she saw that hoodlum coming in her direction. She moved back. "He is about to eat me up!" She closed the window, then she bolted it and remained inside.,

That night, she said to her husband, "*You* don't look at married women, do you?"

"Good lord, I don't' look at anyone! Why this suspiciousness?"

"Maybe you don't look around, but others do!" she said angrily.

"Who?"

Misri could not speak.

The next day she saw that hoodlum again. He turned his head to look up at the house. Misri hid as she watched him.

"That man has swallowed me up!" she said slowly.

Today she didn't bolt the window; she forgot, and just sat in her room. When someone entered her room, she was so startled she jumped up, and almost screamed, but then she saw it was Seti.

Seti said, "Why were you so scared?"

Misri's heart was still beating loudly. She said, "I just wondered who it was!"

Seti spoke of this and that for a while, then said, "Who is that man out there who keeps watching the house—sometimes from one side, sometimes from the other?" Misri turned red, as if she were a thief caught red-handed. "Who?"

"I wonder who! The shopkeeper there said he heard that character was no good. Who knows where that thug is from?"

Misri pulled herself together and, without looking at Seti's face, said, "Maybe he's chasing after my husband's niece."

"Who knows?"

Just as he did every day, her husband returned from the office and sat down to eat *chiura*. She could not speak with him. She was anxious to say something that would be proof of her innocence in this matter, but she could not articulate her feeling. Moreover, she was afraid that if she brought it up, the mystery she was concealing would come out. She could not speak. Later, when her husband was smoking his hookah in the room, she came downstairs while the rice was cooking. She still could not speak, could find no words, and she was still afraid that the mystery she concealed would be revealed. At night, she hurried to finish her chores, but she somehow did not manage to finish them no matter how much work she did. She felt that if she were unable to bring up this matter quickly, she would never be able to do so, which would certainly lead to calamity.

At last she finished her work, and entered their room. However she could not speak now. Her husband turned over a document from his office. The boss had said that this was important work, so he had to do it at home and take it back to the office the next day.

Misri looked at her husband, looked at the twisted shape of his body as he examined the document. It seemed to Misri that his weakness was hidden inside that crooked body. As she watched, she felt full of compassion and kindness. Now it seemed to her that she would not be able to reveal the mystery within her, she would not bring it out. She blurted out, "What interest would someone have in looking at someone else's wife?"

"Who?" her husband asked, without taking his eyes from the paper.

"That hoodlum."

"Who?" Now her husband raised his eyes from the paper and looked at Misri with suspicion and fear.

"You don't know?"

She felt like scratching out her husband's eyes which, fearful with cowardice, were pleading with her.

"That man named Hiraman!" she said. She wanted to see how much cowardice was in those eyes. Now that unkind laugh began to play on her lips.

"Oh—that one," her husband said gently. He was silent a moment and said, "Yes, that one is bad. Yes, I constantly see him in the street. But..."

"But," he continued hurriedly, "It's possible he just happened to come here. You can't tell someone not to walk in the street. Doesn't he have the right to walk in the street? You are frightened."

Misri felt like screaming "No!' but she said nothing, and she continued to look at the crooked body of her husband as he lowered his eyes to examine the document.

"Couldn't you chase him away from the street here?" she asked.

"How?" He looked up from the papers at Misri. "Why?"

"You ask 'why?' To chase him away."

"How?"

"Get some others and do it together."

Her husband only smiled dismissively, and Misri burned with anger. She said, "In that case, you can't do it?"

Her husband now said, "If I did as you asked, we would only disgrace ourselves. If you're afraid, you should be more careful."

"In that case, just say that he would kill you."

After a moment, she said, "If I could just be a man..."

Her husband said nothing. Misri got ready for bed. She said nothing further. She felt so detached that she didn't even feel capable of compassion for her husband's humble eyes. Then she felt her husband move closer to her. He took her hand and said, "Maybe he came to see my niece."

"No."

"Who, then?"

"Me." Misri fearlessly looked at her husband.

Misri saw that her husband's eyes were burning with jealousy. That made her happy, but then as she watched, that jealousy faded, and Misri's face fell. Her husband said, "When you go out, you should take two or three people along—who knows what that hoodlum has planned or what he will do. You must be careful. You mustn't go out by yourself."

Misri looked at her husband with pity.

Her husband took her hand and toyed with it. He said, "Probably he doesn't know that you are married, that you are a daughter-in-law of this house."

Misri now smiled derisively, and again looked at him with pity. She did not take her hand from her husband's grasp.

In a moment she was in her husband's embrace, and she said, with her hand wrapped around her husband's shoulder, "What does he think I am? I am not a weakling!"

She tried to entangle herself tightly around her husband's shoulders, as if someone were pulling at her and she didn't want to go, as if she were trying to reject her own wishes and didn't want to separate from him.

The next day, Misri asked Seti in the kitchen, "Was that hoodlum walking in the street again today?"

"Yes. I saw him turn to look at me again and again. He wanted to speak with me, but I ignored him."

"What would you do if he called to you on the street?" Misri said after a bit, while scrubbing the *puja* vessels.

"I wouldn't say anything."

"If he took your hand?"

"I would spit in his face. I'd shame him in the street!"

Misri giggled, and was surprised at the sound of her own laughter. Seti could not laugh. Misri said to her in a pained voice, "Seti, could you tell him not to bother us?"

Seti looked at her suspiciously, and said, "Why must I speak to him? He'll figure it out when I go to the window and dump the piss from the chamber pot on his head!"

Now Misri could not laugh. As she cleaned the small *puja* bell, she said, "Does everyone in the neighborhood know about this? Do they say that hoodlum comes to see me—I mean us?"

"Not only are they talking—there are rumors."

Misri felt like a criminal as she looked at Seti and said, "We haven't done anything wrong, have we?"

Seti gave no reply, and looked at her face. Seti's eyes seemed to say, "Your beauty has led him on."

Misri said nothing. Having finished scrubbing the *puja* vessels, she went into her mother-in-law's room to sit. It seemed that her mother-in-law spoke sighingly, with love and affection, and not a single burning ember of jealousy was evident. She began to look at her mother-in-law gratefully, as if that amount of love and affection were more than enough for her, as if she didn't deserve so much. Her mother-in-law said gently, "This time I think I won't last. Whatever happens, don't let me die in bed. Carry me to the *ghat* by the river."

Misri could not say anything. If she said something, she would cry. She ran away to her room. She took up the broom to sweep, and just then saw an envelope, a letter which had been left on the carpet in the middle of the room. As she picked up the envelope to put it in a better place, her eyes fell on the handwriting on the envelope, and she sat down, dumbfounded. "Misri" was written on the envelope, and the handwriting was that of the hoodlum. She looked all about. The window shutter was open just a little. The letter from him had been thrown into the room through the window. The handwriting on the envelope dazzled her eyes, so she closed them. The handwriting was trying to play a joke with her emotions; it seemed to her the handwritten letters were jumping about. She tore up the envelope without looking at it, and after she tore it up the room became very quiet.

As she started to go outside the room, she felt relieved, very well. She had not looked at the letter, so she was not immoral. She stood stock still for a moment, and then thought she would go tell this to her husband. She imagined the spark of jealousy in her husband's eyes, and she smiled.

When her husband came home from the office, he was happy. Misri was speechless when she saw him. The department head at his office had been transferred, and her husband had been proposed as department head in his place, a promotion. His boss had confirmed the submission of his name to the minister's office, together with a recommendation. He had certainly pleased his boss; he would only have to go wait on the boss at his home. If required, he would go to wait at the minister's house on two or three days.

Misri could not join in her husband's excitement; she could not counterfeit happiness. She watched her husband in astonishment, thinking "How did he get to be so happy in one day?" The handwriting on the envelope of the letter was mocking her, and she was terrified. It seemed to her that if the matter of the letter were to escape her lips, then it would snuff out all of her husband's happiness and joy in a moment. She did not speak.

Her husband looked at her with alarm and asked, "Why are you so quiet?"

Misri looked at him with pity. It seemed to her that she must say something; saying nothing would result in some difficulty. She said, "You should go to your boss's house, until you get the promotion, just to be sure."

"Yes, of course I'll go. How could I not go?"

At night, pacing in her room, there was no change in Misri's face—it remained serious. She tried to look happy, but she was so tired she was incapable of any sham.

Her husband now became quite worried and said, "What if someone above appoints someone else, someone who has been attending to him more?'

Misri felt as if she would scream, "They can't do that!" But she still could not speak. After a moment, her husband said, "What can we do if that happens? But the boss says not to worry; he will try his best."

Misri peeked for a moment at her husband's steady eyes, and in her mind she decided that she would not speak about the letter.

The next day, as she was cooking the rice, Misri hurriedly left the kitchen. Her period had started. Her insides felt brittle and dry; she felt empty and hollow. She had but one basis for remaining in this household: her womb, which prevented her from being free. She became quiet, and stood leaning against the wall. Later she became frightened and looked wildly about, as if she would stagger and fall.

After some time, her husband came out of the *puja* room. Misri looked at him with hatred. Her husband smiled and asked, "What's wrong? What happened? Your period?"

Misri said nothing.

"In that case, I'll have to do the cooking myself," her husband said.

Misri left the kitchen.

The afternoon seemed very quiet except for the sound of two or three isolated people walking in the street. It seemed to Misri that there was no one in the house except herself; it was very empty. She had pulled the door shut and bolted it from inside; likewise the windows were pulled shut and bolted. She looked all around the room. It looked as if all the things in the room were trying to wake up. She turned over—she didn't really feel sleepy—and she heard someone knocking at the door. She got up suddenly and her heart nearly stopped. "What if it's that man, and my mother-in-law hears him from upstairs?" The knocking at the door continued unabated. She asked angrily, "Who is it?"

The voice of a boy sounded from outside. "Me! Open the door. *Saheb* sent me."

Misri did not know if she felt better or hopeless. She slowly opened the door. The boy flung a letter down and quickly ran down the stairs. She recognized the boy as the neighborhood bully who fought with everyone. Misri picked up the letter.

She looked for a moment at the handwriting on the envelope. It was like the handwriting on the first letter, and the handwriting said, "To my Misri." She was not so shocked as yesterday. The letters did not blur in front of her eyes and did not try to tease her. Rather, it seemed to her that the suffocated voice of the handwriting soothed her feelings. Feeling completely indifferent, she shut up the door to her room. She tore open the letter and read it. The letter was very long, and he had written of many things. She understood half of the things in the letter, and half she didn't understand. It seemed that the whole feeling of the letter soothed her heart. When she read the last sentence, however, her eyes were startled, "A letter will arrive every day until you send a reply." After she read that, she tore up the letter.

Since there was no one to cook the meal, Seti had gone to call her husband's niece, who soon arrived. Misri felt relieved, as if she had been awaiting her arrival for several days. She looked at the niece gratefully, as if she were protection against all her adversity and distress, a bulwark against danger. Now Misri would go to her parents' house and that hoodlum would not follow. If he tormented her with letters there, she would write him. If that didn't work, she would send word. She would write asking him not to bother her like this. She would meet him in person and tell him not to torment her. She would say, "I am married. To court a married woman like this... it's a sin to undermine her principles."

Her husband's niece was irritable as she cooked the rice. She said to Misri, "I have no peace of mind anywhere. I'm so unlucky! At home, too, I can't sit down for even a minute! Everyone is sick just when

I think they are all well, they get sick again immediately!"

Misri said nothing. She was afraid that if she said something, her niece might get angry and go home.

The next day she sat in her room, just like the day before. If somebody brought a letter today, she must prevent it from getting into someone else's hands, so she waited. "What is Hiraman worth?" she thought. But then she was surprised at herself. At what time had he stopped being the "hoodlum" and started being "Hiraman" with the smiling eyes, the fine clothes, his own personality? Even then, she repeated again and again to herself, "That hoodlum! He's worthless!" At last it seemed that she had pulled herself out of her reverie, and she felt relieved. Then she thought, "That neighborhood kid is worthless!" She sat, waiting for the letter.

Evening began to fall. Her husband had returned from the office, but the letter had not come. Even though she was having her period, it was permissible to slice the vegetables and do some sweeping. She went upstairs to the kitchen. As she was slicing up the vegetables, she began to have doubts: what if that worthless boy had thrown the letter into her room? She stopped cutting up the vegetables and went downstairs. Her husband was sitting in the usual place smoking his tobacco in the hookah, just as he did every day. Even though her husband was there, it seemed as if the room were empty. She hesitated for a moment, watching her husband smoke. At that time there was a commotion in the street. Misri stepped over to the window on the area of the floor from which the carpet had been turned over, as a woman having her period is not permitted to walk on the carpets. The noise of a demonstration rose in the distance. Gradually the words "Long live...! Long live...!" were distinguishable. People had come out of their houses into the lane asking "What's the demonstration about?" and were running up to see. Misri watched from the window, and saw flags and placards going by up on the main street. Misri thought that this could be the reason the letter hadn't come. But then she suddenly thought, "Maybe the police arrested Hiraman and took him away!" She looked anxiously at her husband's face.

Her husband, indifferent to the demonstration, was absorbed in his smoking. Misri turned away her face in disgust.

After a moment, her husband asked, "Is there a big crowd?"

Misri did not speak. After the street became quiet, she thought, "It would be better if they arrested him and took him away."

She asked her husband, "Do they arrest the demonstrators and take them away?"

"We have a democracy. Why would they arrest them?" her husband answered.

Misri hesitated; she could not figure out whether she felt well or ill.

On the third day of her period, Misri saw from the window that the corrupt boy had entered the ground floor of the house. Misri confusedly went downstairs. The boy, grinning, gave her another letter. She tried to say something, but she couldn't. So she took the letter, and went upstairs into her room.

In this letter, as in the previous one, he wrote of many things, and at the end he had written, "Yesterday and the day before, it was not convenient to send a letter, but I still haven't received a reply from you. You could give a reply to the boy who brought you the letter. I will keep sending a letter every day until I get a response."

"Will you write a reply for me?" She smiled a little. She would not write a letter. She would not commit a sin like that. She thought, "Who is he, that I should write a letter?"

She put the letter in its envelope and firmly decided that she would go to her parents' house after her bath the next morning without fail. It seemed to her that every moment pulled her toward this disaster, and time was passing. If she didn't take advantage of time, everything would be ruined. Yes, she must do something quickly. Even if she had to rant and rave, she must make that Hiraman hoodlum leave her alone. She would have to say to her parents' neighbor Ramman, "How have I misled all of you? How could you torment me like this?"

The next day, after doing the purification rites for the end of her period, Misri said to her mother-in-law, "Mother, after I've finished the cooking, I'll go to my parents' house."

Her mother-in-law was rested. She said, "If you have to go, go. You might not come back again today. I can't depend on any of you."

Misri said nothing. The niece was in doubt. Misri said, "Ill come back today after I've had my bath. Why do you doubt me?"

Misri took formal leave of her husband after he had finished eating his rice.

Her husband was perhaps in his room, getting dressed to go to the office; Misri hurriedly went downstairs. She wanted to see her husband's face. She returned after going as far as the door. "I'll be gone for a short time today..."

"Why?" asked her husband.

"I'll come back later today," Misri said to herself. She thought to herself that she didn't want to come back.

"I'll come back later today," she said in a loud voice. But it seemed to her that she might never see her husband again.

"What predicaments there are in life! I could die, or something else could happen there." She returned again to look at her husband's face. Her husband put on his coat and his shoes. Smiling, he said, "Why are you looking at me like that?"

"Just because!" Misri turned her face away.

In the afternoon, when Misri had dressed to go to her parent's house, she sat down on her heels. She suddenly didn't want to go. Seti said, "It's late. I'll have the pots to clean when I come back..."

Misri thought, "As soon as I get there, I'll send for Ramman."

But what pretext could she use to call for him? She began to worry. Seti said, "What are you doing? It's late!"

"I need an excuse to send for him. Then I'll return here later," she thought.

She put on her shoes to go.

Chapter Four

IN the midst of the bustling main road, Misri's smothered breast felt a semblance of freedom, as if the fog tightly clogging her breast had dissipated. A young man stared at her fixedly; after she had passed him she quickly checked her sari, and her embroidered shawl. They proved to be in place, but then she thought that perhaps she had forgotten to comb her hair. She ran her hand over her hair to check, and found that she had indeed combed it. How stupid! She smiled a little.

As she walked on, she came to an abrupt halt. That insolent boy who had brought her the letter was rolling a hoop, playing *Chakali Paen Paen.* Startled, Misri recalled that she had forgotten to think of this matter. If that boy were to bring a letter today, into whose hands would it fall? Misri and that boy's eyes spoke to one another. Her eyes said, "Look, I'm going away today," and the boy's eyes said, "Yes, I understand."

Misri walked hurriedly, as it seemed to her that the people in the street were looking at her and that boy with hatred and criticism. Seti said, "Why do we have to walk so fast?"

When she reached the neighborhood of her parents' house, Misri stood looking at her own family house and the house opposite. Sunlight had reached the lowest window of the other house, and her parents' house was in the shade. Misri halted for a moment. It seemed to her that those two houses were talking to one another.

Seti said, "What's wrong?"

Misri said, "Nothing—just something stuck on my foot."

Then she felt very upset, as she just remembered something she had forgotten. She was going to call Ramman and ask him a favor, and if he refused she had to be prepared for a quarrel: this was what she had forgotten to think about. She very quickly stepped forward, but just as quickly she froze—what if she met Hiraman here on the road? As if the ghost of Hiraman were pursuing her, she hurriedly entered her parents' house. Seti said, "What's the matter with you?"

Misri, her face turning red, said, "Nothing's wrong!"

Seti looked all around the road from the door. There was nothing there, only people walking in the road and shopkeepers sitting in their shops as usual. After that, she looked at Misri as if to dispel the mystery, but Misri said nothing, and turned her head away.

As Misri climbed the stairs she felt at last that she had reached the safety of her mother's lap. When she reached the upper floor she stood still to rest. The environment of love and affection filled her breast. She drew a long sigh, and pulled on the closed door of her father's room.

"Father isn't here?" she asked in a loud voice.

"Eh, he *is* here," she answered herself.

Seti, climbing the stairs behind her, asked, "Why are you talking to yourself?"

Misri awoke from her self-absorption. Embarrassed, she turned her head and said, "I asked if Father was in."

She went upstairs and formally greeted her mother. Her mother said, "I'm glad you came! I was thinking about sending for you, but today there was no one to send. There is so much work to do here! How can I do all this by myself? There are only four days left until the *Shraddha* ceremony. Your sister-in-law went to her parents' house yesterday, and says she'll come back tomorrow. You see? I even have to cook the meals! Your sister-in-law had an invitation somewhere, so she had to go. She could have gone from here, too."

Misri said, "I have to go back later today."

Her mother looked at her daughter for a moment in disbelief. "What did you say? And with so much work? The quilt cover has been sewn but not put together. I am alone to do all this work. We have to get everything together for *Shraddha*. The leaf-plates have to be stitched together."

"No, I said I would be back later today."

"Can't you stay here? With all this work..."

Misri turned her face away. In a moment her breast welled up and her eyes filled with tears. She said in a hollow voice, "I said I would come back later when I left."

Her mother could not say anything. She looked, surprised, at Misri's reaction, and after a moment said, "All right, if you have to go, go—if you said you would go back. What I thought was that one day... Did you eat before you came?"

Misri signaled "yes" by shaking her head, and turned her face away. Her mother's feelings were shining from her eyes, just as they had when Misri was small. In a moment, the feelings in those eyes had changed. Now it seemed those eyes were saying, "If you were still small, I'd take you on my lap and kiss you, but now you've grown up, and the daughter I raised belongs to others." Misri again turned her face away. Her eyes again filled with tears.

It seemed to her that the whole house was a conscious being, who wanted to wrap her in a blanket, and hold her in its lap. But no, she wanted to be free from those bonds of love, she wanted to be free from that lap.

"Today I must return," she thought; she had to leave her mother's side. Then she thought again. "If I don't return today, I won't be able to return, ever." She walked hurriedly, as if she wanted to escape from that temptation.

After a moment she was surprised to realize that she had completely forgotten about the task that she had come to do. She must send for the neighbor Ramman now, right now. But how should she call him, and what should she say? She began to worry. She must send to speak with him. Why should she feel any awe of him, any shame? At that time she seemed to glimpse that hoodlum Hariman making a sign with his hand: "Come, come!" Without realizing it she raised her hand to make a request. She wanted to say, "I've got a request. Please don't follow me. Don't give me a bad reputation. Don't push me into hell. What have I done to you?"

"Did you just arrive?"

Misri came to and got up. Her father was in front of her. She said, "Yes," and gave him a formal greeting.

"Didn't you arrange it so you wouldn't have to go back?"

"I have to go back!" she said, but it seemed to Misri that she would not be able to go back. She felt very upset as she realized that if too much time passed, everything would be ruined. She had to make a decision fast, and she had to get in touch with that Ramman. If not, she must write a letter. While her father talked of other things, she just replied "yes" and "no" by shaking her head. She was thinking how she would put it to Ramman in a letter.

"If I were to write that letter, what then?" she said to herself.

Her father asked, "Aren't' you well? What's wrong?"

Misri felt very embarrassed as she came to. She quickly said, "Yes, it's just that my head..."

"In that case, how can you go back?"

"There is no one else there," she said, becoming calm.

After her father left, she decided that she must do something immediately. She would do something and think later. She tried not to worry, and thought that not now but after some time she would console herself.

Now, Misri tried to make herself feel natural while descending the stairs. Pretending to be displeased, she said, "Mother, why didn't you send me that sari I asked for the day before yesterday?"

Her mother said, "Oh, I forgot! and besides there was no one to take it."

Misri said in a pouting voice, "You always say that. You could have sent it with anybody."

Misri started to leave the room. Her mother said, "Wait, where are you going? Stay here!"

Misri saw that today her mother really wanted to talk. For many days her mother had been unable to spill out all the thoughts welling up within her. There was no one to listen patiently—everyone either just laughed at her, or got angry. As her mother's parents were poor, her mother did not want to burden her parents and elder brother when she went to visit them. When she did go there, she didn't stay long.

Her mother said, "And so your father and your brothers treat me badly. They don't pay any attention to me and turn up their noses."

Her mother started talking to Misri about her younger brother's marriage. The prospective bride's parents were from good families, but for some unknown reason, Misri's father did not like the girl. Well, he liked the girl, but didn't like the mother and father. They seemed too self-important to him. As for her brother, he wanted to choose his own wife and didn't want to marry someone his parents chose. He wanted an educated girl. Her mother had said that one married a woman, not an education. Her mother could accept his desire to have a fine girl—and that girl was adequate. If you want an angel, you'll never get one here on earth; such can only be found in the realms of the gods! They wanted someone from a good family, and she was indeed from a good family!

"A good family?" When those words collided with Misri's brain she could not tolerate it. She laughed ironically. Now she wanted to jeer at herself along with her mother. A crooked smile danced on her face.

Her mother, gaining steam, said, "Even if she's not so good-looking, so what? Do you marry a face? If she has a good nature, then marry her. They teased me for saying that. And your older brother—he agrees with your younger brother!"

Misri kept smiling. Her mother said angrily, "Why are you smiling? You are like the others! I will not give up on bringing that girl here! Right away!"

"What do I care?" said Misri.

"What do I care, she says!" Her mother stared at her. "All right, no one cares about my troubles."

"Why are you taking this trouble? Let him take care of his own happiness."

Immediately, it seemed as if someone had thrown a stick at Misri: no, what she said wasn't right; no one had a right to his own happiness.

"I shouldn't take the trouble? If I don't take the trouble who would? If I hadn't taken the trouble would your marriage have come so soon? If I hadn't taken the trouble, you would have ended up with that drunk, the one who killed his wife in a drunken fit," she said.

Misri's face reacted in horror. She sought to reply with bitter words—words that would be a slap in her mother's face—but she could not think of the right words, and after a few moments of bewilderment, she felt empty.

Her mother started to talk about other things. She herself had to do every little thing in the household. Misri's father had become as simple and naive as Ganesh. If she asked him something, he was just irritable; he didn't care about anything. Her older brother was satisfied with just getting good food. Her younger brother went to school, came home, and then stayed out until night.

Misri was aghast at hearing this mockery of good fortune. She had not been married off to that drunkard; instead, she got married to Haribhakta, with whom she was bound together until death. This had happened merely because her mother had taken the trouble. "If mother hadn't taken the trouble..." she thought. "If mother had not been there..." She completed the thought: she would have married that drunkard, and she would have been beaten, beaten to death, instead of that other woman. She would never have been able to come to her parents' house, and that hoodlum would never have seen her, and she would not have to endure this torment now.

Her mother said, "Look at your sister-in-law! She has never swept my room, not once!"

Misri's words suddenly broke out, "Why did you take the trouble to arrange my marriage?"

Her mother stared at her in surprise, and Misri came to; her mother's talk had already taken an altogether different direction.

"Today I must bring this matter to a close," she thought, and for some time she wandered from room to room, upstairs and downstairs. "I need to finish this matter right now." She entered her own bedroom and opened the window. Sunlight was hanging on the window of that room in the house opposite. That room looked very quiet, and she could almost see the furnishing beyond the curtain in the window. She looked far, far up the road—there was no one to be seen. She looked for that girl who had brought the letter the first time she had been at her parents' house, but she was not playing or walking around anywhere. A porter walked by carrying a load; his naked chest could be seen beneath his torn tunic. Then she saw a girl coming, and she wanted that girl to be the one who had brought the letter. "It's the same girl," she said to herself, then "No, it's not that girl," she answered herself, and for a long time she kept saying "Yes", then "No."

The curtain in that window in the house opposite was pulled aside. Misri jumped up from where she was sitting, but it was a woman who came to stand in the window. Ramman's wife looked at Misri and smiled, but Misri did not smile in return, and turned her face away as if she didn't know her. "Let her think I'm a snob—I don't care," Misri thought. She would deal with each and every person in that house in the same manner. She would not know anyone in that house. They had all joined in a scheme to try to ruin and defile her. She would ignore all the people in that house, even if they were to die. If that house were suddenly to collapse into a pile of rubble, she would laugh and dance. If they asked for help, she would curse them even more. She felt better after she had imagined these events.

When the sun set and evening fell, Misri was dismayed to realize that she still had not accomplished what she had come to do, and that she would return to her husband's house just as she had come here, without bringing this matter to a conclusion. She could not understand what she had been doing while so much time went by. It wasn't that she had not tried to meet Ramman, but she had not so much as seen him. "Where did he disappear to?" she wondered. When she saw her younger brother Ramesh come into the house, she ran out so she could send him to call Ramman. But when she got to Ramesh, no words came forth.

Ramesh said, "Did you get here during the day? And you're going back today?"

Misri said, "Yes, I'm going back."

She still could not tell him to go call Ramman. She brought up the subject of marriage.

"Why did you say you're not getting married?"

"Because I don't like her."

"Whom do you like, then?"

"What do all of you care? There is somebody. Should I just be like all of you, and marry whoever someone gives me? Should I consult the astrological signs?"

Misri could not smile. She looked at Ramesh.

"I don't' care about caste. I don't care about lineage or family," said Ramesh.

Misri thought she should scold him soundly, but she could not speak.

"I want an educated, beautiful wife who will understand my mind," Ramesh continued.

Her mother came along at that point. Pretending to be angry, she said, "Misri, listen to what your brother is saying! He's not even ashamed! I'll rip off his face, for being such a smart-aleck..."

Misri still couldn't smile.

That night, as she was eating, her mother said, "Oh, your uncle brought some mango pickle from the plains. I saved some for you. Wait, don't eat your rice too fast and I'll bring some to you."

When her mother had hurriedly brought the pickle and put it on Misri's plate, she felt a wave of emotion, and tears threatened to drown her eyes. She put her head down so that no one would see her in this state. The love her mother gave her was more than she could possibly return. She sighed, and after a moment pretending the hot pickles made her nose sting and tears well up, she pinched her nose and raised her head.

In the midst of eating her meal, she stopped. Perhaps Seti had come to take her home. Maybe she was on the road, and about to reach here, and Misri would have to go home without finishing her business. Finally, it looked as if she would not see Ramman, nor would she see that hoodlum Hiraman. No, if that business were not finished, and she went home to her husband, the whole thing would never be finished. And Hiraman would continue to follow her, until that horrible thing would happen. She stopped eating and stood up.

"Why are you throwing good food away?" asked her mother.

"I don't feel like eating."

While she was on the ledge-like verandah next to the kitchen, washing her hands and rinsing her mouth, she had a glimpse of herself toppling off the edge; she felt that if she didn't pull herself together she would fall and be smashed like a cup falling from the roof.

Later, when Seti came to take her back, she had decided, and decided firmly. Seti, surprised, said, "Today is *Shraddha,* the memorial puja. You bathed today, of course."

Misri, pretending to be a non-believer, laughed and said, "Why? Nowadays, it is not practical to bathe every day. Before, when I got sick two or three times, I did not bother bathing before returning home. If I did that, why should I bathe every day?"

"It would be all right if you didn't wash your head."

"And why should I wash everything, even including my head?"

Seti could not argue. After a moment, she said, "Who will cook the rice? Will the master cook it himself? He has to go to the office—what a state he'll be in. And Niece has to go home tomorrow."

Misri suddenly giggled, thinking of her husband sitting at the hearth, surrounded by smoke, trying to start a fire that wouldn't start. Seti looked at her, startled. Misri could not stop laughing. The laughter began to assume frightening proportions. Seti shrieked, "Why are you laughing?"

Misri became silent just as suddenly as she had started laughing.

That day, no matter how much pressure Seti exerted, Misri refused to return. "If my mother-in-law gets angry for three or four days, what then? And then, if my husband has problems for three or four days, so what?" she thought. The anger of her mother-in-law and the troubles of her husband were less important than a danger which would turn her life upside down. As soon as she faced them again, her other-in-law's anger would subside, and her husband would be happy.

The next morning sunlight fell on the roof of the house opposite just as before. The cat slowly emerged from the attic window, and crept toward a nearby pigeon. Misri, full of anxiety, breathlessly watched the cat's evil deed. The pigeon was absorbed in eating the offerings scattered around the roof. The cat pounced, and Misri covered her eyes. When she took her hands away from her eyes, she watched as the cat, with dead pigeon clamped in its mouth, jumped into the attic window. She thought of Hiraman and laughed at how he and the cat acted in the same way. Ramman's mother appeared in the attic window, and scattered rice offerings to Suryanarayan, the sun god. The pigeons and sparrows hesitated to pick up those scattered offerings, and Misri felt pleased at their cautiousness. The sunlight slowly moved, coloring the upper floor of the house. Then again, slowly the sunlight advanced until it was hanging on the window where that hoodlum Hiraman came to sit. The sunlight fell upon the photos that were in that room opposite, and their shining reflection returned to the room in which Misri was sitting. Today, up to now, no one had appeared, including that Hiraman; nor was that girl who had brought the letter walking about anywhere. Misri thought: yet another two or three days remain, during which this matter would be decided. Then that Hiraman would stop following her. She laughed to think that he could even now be loitering around her husband's house.

Misri looked up into the clear sky, where an eagle was soaring, free of care. She thought she heard a sound, so she looked downward at the street. Now, she was shocked speechless, numbed by what she saw: that Hiraman was with her brother Ramesh, and they were walking toward the house! Hiraman's face was playful, and he was joking as usual. Misri stiffened as she sat in the window. Then she froze as she heard footsteps on the stairs; terrified, she got up and rushed out of the room. She ran to the kitchen, then fled to the roof terrace, where she paced back and forth. "He's made friends with Ramesh!" she said to herself.

After pacing back and forth for some time, she calmed down. "I must bring this matter to an end today," she thought, and her legs began to tremble. She sat down. After a while she thought again: "Not now, not immediately. I'll take care of it by speaking to Ramman. If that doesn't work, I'll write a letter."

She went downstairs. Seeing her sister-in-law in the kitchen, she asked, "Did you just arrive?"

"What did you say?" Her sister-in-law was startled by the unnatural expression in Misri's face.

Misri pulled herself together and said, "Eh, that's right, you came this morning."

Ramesh appeared at the door of the kitchen. Misri's legs again began to tremble.

Ramesh said, "Sister-in-law, please make some tea. Today I'm going to the movies. A friend of our neighbor Ramman, whose name is Hiraman, is downstairs."

Her sister-in-law, astonished, looked at Misri. Misri stared at her sister-in-law like a criminal, as if she wanted to say, "I didn't knowingly do anything shameful, Sister-in-law!"

Ramesh felt that something was unnatural and looked at the two of them one by one for a moment, "Why? What's wrong?"

Misri turned her face away. Sister-in-law said, "Nothing's wrong."

Ramesh said, "If Sister-in-law has other work, my sister could make the tea—that might be better."

"What's that?" Misri turned her head back. She peered at Ramesh as if she were trying to under-standing him. "I'm not here to make tea or whatever for anybody!"

"He bought me a ticket to the movies. I thought that at least I could bring him a cup of tea," said Ramesh, modestly.

Misri felt pity for Ramesh and looked at him as if to say, "Please listen to my request, Ramesh—don't accept that movie ticket."

Ramesh went downstairs. After a bit the sound of boiling water filled the kitchen. Misri's sister-in-law set the water aside and, as she was busy cleaning the rice, asked Misri to make the tea.

Misri looked angrily at her sister-in-law, who seemed to be trying to read her mind. "All right, give it to me. I'll make it."

As Misri made the tea, she said to herself, "Should I serve the tea as well? Is there any reason I should fear that person?"

At that point Ramesh came upstairs and asked, "How much time does it take to do something simple like make tea?"

Misri said, "You two are not such great rajas that tea can be prepared at your command!"

Misri watched as Ramesh took the two cups of tea from her in his own hands and managed by him-self. She felt helpless when the cups were taken away. She watched as Ramesh disappeared from the kitchen door. The sound of his footsteps gradually faded as he descended the stairs.

The rhythmic sound of her sister-in-law winnowing the rice in a flat basket kept up for a while, then stopped. The dust from the bran filled the kitchen and tinged the air with color, lingering in the beams of light next to the window. Misri stirred as if to run out of the kitchen, but she was frozen with fear. Would her sister-in-law guess that she was setting off downstairs to see Hiraman? But it seemed to Misri that her sister-in-law was affecting not to notice, and was pretending to be absorbed in her work.

"If sister-in-law thinks that, so what? Let her think—I'm going!" she thought angrily, and went downstairs. She reached her own room, and listened attentively for sounds from the room below, where Ramesh and Hiraman were sitting. But not a sound could be heard, and she had the delusion that someone nearby was sighing. She got up decisively and went to the stairs that led down. An impulse to keep going pushed her onwards. She must hear what those two were saying, must hear. But she stopped herself, and stood still.

"If he becomes friends with Ramesh, Ramesh will be corrupted," she thought, and seemed to feel some support for her impulses. Then she thought, "I must strongly advise Ramesh."

After a moment she again felt unable to resist the strong desire to eavesdrop. "What are those two talking about?" But again she stopped herself.

"Ramesh is my younger brother, so I must guide him," she said to herself.

After some time she heard Ramesh and Hiraman go down the stairs. Misri quickly returned to her room and stood in the window. Hiraman, deliberately showing that he wasn't looking up, kept his arm around Ramesh's shoulder as they walked away.

It seemed to Misri that Hiraman was deliberately showing her that he was not a bad person—rather, how good, how sincere! Misri smiled.

When evening fell and the rooms of the house were covered in darkness, Misri felt alarmed. During the entire day, even thought she was to do that certain task, she hadn't finished it. The matter was still right where she had left it. That hoodlum Hiraman had even come to her own home, and she still had not concluded the matter. There had been one stairway's distance between her and that man, but she had been unable to approach him. While Ramesh had gone up to the kitchen, she could have gone quietly into the room where he was alone. Angrily, she could have said anything she wanted to say. She could even have scolded him, and if he hadn't listened, she could have requested him not to bother her. It would have been good even if she had cried. She had let this opportunity slip by. Even if she had gone in the room when Ramesh was there, who would have stopped her? If she had told Ramesh not to get mixed up with this worthless hoodlum, Hiraman would have been insulted, and left of his own accord. If he refused to leave, she could have got rid of him by screaming. She had let this opportunity escape from her fingers.

"But how could it have been?" she asked herself after a moment.

That night Seti came again to call her. Misri did not have the courage to face her again, and she wanted to run away where no one would find her.

"You can't *not* go today. Your mother-in-law was extremely angry. Why is everyone pouring anger on me? Everyone jumps on me!"

Misri no longer had the courage to look at Seti's face, and lowered her head as she asked, "Is he angry also?"

"Who? Oh... the master? Who can understand his mind? I don't know if he's angry or not. He hasn't spoken. But your mother-in-law told him, 'Since you've become such a silent simpleton everyone despises you.'"

Misri could not smile. She must not flinch in her determination not to go. She had not accomplished even one iota of that matter for which she had deceived them in order to come to her parents' house. She now looked at Seti's face and said, "Not today, no, Seti. Please, the day after tomorrow. Tomorrow will be Tuesday; tomorrow is an inauspicious day."

Just then her mother joined them and, motioning to Seti, she said, "There are only four or five days left until *Shraddha*, and all the preparations have to be made. My daughter should leave only after *Shraddha*. What can be done?"

And then her mother plied Seti with all kinds of reasons. Seti made some objections, but after a bit she admitted defeat and descended the stairs. Her mother called out to Seti from her room, "Tell my son-in-law not to be late for *Shraddha*, eh, Seti!"

The sound of Seti's footsteps faded slowly away. And then, as if Misri had forgotten to tell Seti something, she went to the window. But when she reached the window, she couldn't remember what she had wanted to say. In the soft light cast on the road from the rooms of the houses all around, only the shape of Seti's head could be seen. Her face was not clearly visible. She became smaller and smaller until she was only a speck in the distance. The speck got smaller and disappeared. Then Misri had a feeling of being very empty inside, and with that empty feeling she looked at the areas of the road that were dark, and at the areas that were light. After a moment, an incomprehensible misery, a sickness began to stroke her breast. She left the window. How alone she was. There was no one to help her, and she mustn't ask for help from anyone. She must not go so far as to let anyone know, let alone ask for help. If she were to ask for help, she risked getting a bad reputation, and she would certainly fall in everyone's estimation. She had to work through this enormous problem by herself; she would have to settle it herself without letting anyone know. She was in a dilemma. Sister-in-law knows something, she thought, but she knew only that the hoodlum had targeted her. She did not know about the letters or how far the situation had advanced. She thought that it would have been better if she had gone with Seti. She had an impression that in her husband's house there was some kind of unknown power that would giver her support and take her out of danger. She looked again from the window, but Seti was not there. Perhaps Seti had reached the house by now. Even if she were to sit in the window and yell herself hoarse, Seti would not hear.

The next morning Misri felt weary when she awoke. It seemed to her that all night she had been tossing and turning. As she got up from the bed, she felt in herself the same sense of misery and illness that she had felt the day before—how alone she felt! After some time, she felt the same regret she had felt the night before, and thought how it would have been better to go with Seti. The day passed like the previous day; again she could not do that which she had come to do. Like the day before, she felt certain that there was an unknown power at her husband's house that would strengthen her by giving her support, and protect her from danger. There, that Hiraman's hopes would be dashed, and his desire for her would suddenly desert him.

The whole house was as if enveloped in gloom. When her father came in from shopping, gave her a bag of provisions and said the price was too high, it seemed like a sigh of hopelessness. When her older brother said, "No need to cook a meal for me today—I'm going to a banquet," it seemed to Misri that these words were sounds from the depths of hopelessness. The sight of her mother, filled with love and affection, seemed to Misri to show the hopelessness of separation.

Unexpectedly, her husband's eyes seemed to watch her from some corner, eyes which were mute with passivity and defeat in the face of life. It seemed to her that she was defeated like that, and that her eyes, too, were mute with isolation and sadness. She had a delusion of hearing her husband's soft footsteps, and it seemed that he was fearfully trying to say something. That delusion was real! She sat absorbed in it. After a moment she saw clearly the back of her husband, who had to cook his own food; he had no complaints, only acceptance, as he stooped over the hearth. Her eyes filled with tears of pity.

"Poor thing!" she said to herself.

Then after some time, it seemed to her that the whole house was yawning with laziness; Misri thought she had to do something, that just sitting around quietly would not get her work done. If the girl who had brought the first letter came around she would call her, would send her. She would not write a letter. Whatever she did, she would not write. Unexpectedly, her husband's words came to mind; he had said to someone that "Writing and speaking are not the same, so don't give out anything you've written down to anyone!" She smiled a little.

She went to the window and leaned against the shutters. Without looking at the house opposite, she watched people far away coming and going. After some time her father could be seen from afar on the road. Then again, after some time, she saw Ramesh, smartly dressed, leaving the house.

"What are you looking at?"

Misri jumped. Golsan was standing in front of her, smiling. Golsan often came to the house when there was extra work to do; she scrubbed the pots, went to the shops, summoned people, or did whatever was needed.

"Why, Golsan, where have you been?"

Golsan smiled as before, looked at her and said, "You looked so sad. I wondered what you were looking at."

"Nothing, nothing at all. Just looking," said Misri nervously.

Golsan's face became serious, and she started to say something, but could not manage and fell silent. Misri said, "Do you have something to say to me?"

"Oh, nothing—never mind. Where is your mother?"

"Upstairs."

Golsan looked about the room for a moment, then went out. It seemed to Misri that Golsan did not go upstairs at all, but went back downstairs. After Golsan left, the room became very quiet. Tired from standing so long, Misri sat down and, resting her head against the window, resumed watching the people coming and going in the street. She had the impression that someone was standing in the door, so she turned to look. She rose in confusion, and felt she would scream, but the sound died in her throat. She looked, stiff as a statue. Yes, it was Hiraman. Yes, that was his face, a face filled with passion, that face inflamed with a mixture of courage and fear. Hiraman advanced toward Misri. Misri stood stock-still, watching as if she were about to hand over her soul to death. It was as if that face sighed, and was trying to say something, but she understood nothing. When Hiraman came very close, Misri understood what he was saying. Breathless, he was saying, "You didn't answer my letter?"

Misri's lips trembled, but no sound escaped.

"Tell me—there's no one here—what is there to be afraid of?"

Misri felt her arms being pressed with some force. She again started to scream, but Hiraman's hands were holding her arms.

Misri's words finally escaped. In a tearful voice, she said softly, "Let me go."

"No, I won't let go, not until you give me an answer. Will you go with me or not?"

It seemed to Misri that within the parameter of an instant she had been standing there like that forever. As Hiraman's lips moved and the nervous whispering voice spoke, another endless amount of time passed. Now Hiraman's hot breath was rapidly striking her cheek, and that also seemed to have been happening for an endless amount of time. It seemed to her that something was biting her arm. She said, "ah" softly and looked at the place she'd been bitten. She saw that Hiraman's hand had pinched her.

Hiraman's passionate voice was saying in that whispering voice, "Tell me if you are going or not. I won't leave until you tell me. I won't leave no matter who comes."

Misri now cried in earnest. "Let me go! Someone will come and see us!"

"Say: 'I'll go.'" Hiraman's hand remained firmly on Misri's arm.

Now it seemed to Misri that she heard her mother's voice, and someone was climbing the stairs.

She was panic-stricken, and tried forcefully to release herself from Hiraman's grip. "I'll go, I'll go! Just let go of me!"

In an instant, Hiraman was not there. Misri was stunned. Hiraman's hot breath seemed still to be striking her face. She brushed her arm, as if still trying to release it.

Did that event happen or not? She wanted desperately to understand, to remember. She stood and stared absently. That Hiraman had appeared in the door and had arrived at her side in a flash. That man's hot, quick breath had struck her cheek. He had grabbed her arm, pinched it, and said, "Say: 'I'm going'" and now she brushed her arm, as if she were still trying to release it, as if he were still grasping her arm.

Sister-in-law came in and said, "Why are you staring absent-mindedly like that? Go and eat some *chiura*..

Sister-in-law's face, shadowy and indistinct, now grew clearer. "Yes, this is my sister-in-law." It was as if Misri had just awakened—this was consciousness. And the event that came before? Was that a dream? Misri tried to clear her mind. No, that too was waking consciousness. She sighed, and sat down.

Her sister-in-law said, "Why are you sitting down again?"

Yes, her sister-in-law was reality; what came before was a dream. Misri stood up.

"What are you doing? What's wrong?" her sister-in-law asked.

No, that wasn't a dream either—that was reality. Misri, as if she had forgotten something, looked here and there in the room and then, as if she had suddenly remembered, went to the bureau and opened a drawer.

"It's late," said Sister-in-law, and she looked at Misri sharply for a moment before she went out. Misri felt confused, and she forgot whatever it was she was searching for and shut the drawer.

No, that was not a dream, that was reality. Hiraman had appeared in the door, and had come before her in a flash. His hot, quick breath had fallen on her cheek. He had grabbed her arm and pinched it and she heard "Say: 'I'll go'." She again tried to push the hand away and forcefully brushed her arm. She sat down again.

For one moment it seemed to Misri that all had been a dream, but in the next moment it seemed that all was reality. After that, dream and reality played hide and seek all day so that it seemed that he had drugged her. That night, as she was eating her meal, it seemed to her that she was eating her meal in a dream, so she stopped eating and got up. Later that night she awoke from sleep, crying "No! No!" In a dream, somebody had wrapped her in a black blanket and was abducting her. She was suffocating inside the blanket, and was thrashing about trying to get out.

The room was dark. She pressed the light-switch; the room filled with light. In that moment, the light bulb looked at her in reality. She was still panting, breathing heavily. She looked at all the things in the room—the pictures hanging on the wall, the chest, the bureau—it was as if everything had awakened from sleep. She was wide awake and alert, and her breath returned to normal. The dream she saw in sleep was lost in her subconscious. It seemed to her that she would have to think, would have to think. If she didn't think now, she would never have a chance to think, and the time for doing something about this would have gone by. She looked, and saw that just as the door from which Hiraman had come was real, his breath falling on her cheek as he grabbed her arm and pinched it and said to her "Say: 'I'll go!" was equally real.

"I'll go! I'll go! Just let go of me!" She heard her own voice speaking, and abruptly she stood up. Oh! She had said that, she had said that, and she began to pace back and forth in the room. Her shadow, moving between the light and shadow of the room, terrified her whenever it grew larger and took on a huge shape, touching the rafters. Then her shadow became small and seemed to disappear inside her own body, or beneath her sole. Still she was terrified. After a moment, it seemed to her that no, she hadn't said that. It was just a delusion that she had said that. No, it was not her voice, it was someone else's voice. It was only just like her voice. That was Hiraman's voice, it was his voice.

"No, I didn't say that. I didn't speak." She sat down.

As she sat, that voice in her ear began to sigh, "I'll go, I'll go! Just let go of me!" Yes, she had said that, she could not call back those lingering words. "Oh, Bhagwan! I said that!" she thought, and covered her mouth. Anguish spread through the veins and arteries of her body, and she sobbed, "I am so unlucky! A sinner!" Then she stopped crying and put aside the quilt and said, "I am going home tomorrow. I will not stay here."

Chapter Five

THE crowing of the rooster sometimes seemed to come from far, far away, and sometimes from very near, perhaps from the lower floor of her own house. Misri was submerged in the bottomless depths of sleep, and was unaware that she had fallen asleep. Forgetting all cares and misery, she slept profoundly. Her sleep ended only when it was very light outside. Sunlight pierced the closed window to touch her body. Reflecting for a moment, she sat motionless. A picture of sadness, she worried a moment about whether or not to open the window shutters, and then went out of the room.

As she went to wash her face, she seemed to remember something, but then forgot it. The water was cold. She let the water fall on her feet for a long time. Her feet felt as if they would fall off in the sharp cold. It was a pleasant sensation. She held her hands in the water a long time in the same way. "Today I have to go home," she thought, and stopped washing her face for a moment, contemplating. She had to go—that fact was enough, and there was no need to fabricate another excuse. She put her feet in the water again, as well as her hands.

As she was eating her meal, it seemed to her that the food hesitated in her mouth, moved around, then went down slowly. It seemed to her that she had been eating and eating for a very long time, and that the eating would never be finished. Afterwards, she looked to see if she had finished eating, and for a long time couldn't comprehend whether or not there was any food left. Then she got up.

As she left the kitchen and was descending the stairs, Golsan's sharp eyes were reading her face. Misri said, "What is it, Golsan?"

Golsan said nothing, just followed her.

Misri reached her own room, and suspiciously asked, "What is it, Golsan? Why are you following me without saying anything?"

Golsan hesitated a little, confused, and said, "The master asked when you are going."

Misri, frightened, looked at Golsan, but pulled herself together, as if she didn't understand. She said, "What did you say? What master? I didn't understand."

Golsan, her eyes twinkling, said, "You don't need to fool me. You think I don't know?"

Misri froze with fear. Golsan became serious and said, "Who would I tell? I wouldn't say anything to anyone. Yes, tell me—when are you going?"

Misri stared speechlessly at Golsan. Golsan, as before, said with dancing eyes, "The master thinks of you night and day. I was amazed!"

Misri kept looking at Golsan's round face, where her two small eyes were dancing. Misri wanted to rip out those two eyes.

Just then, they heard the sound of Misri's father climbing the stairs. The footsteps gradually came closer, and it seemed to Misri that she would be caught, so she moved closer to the wall of the room. The sound of her father's footsteps came to the door and stopped. Misri was glued to the wall, and she turned her head away to avoid looking at her father.

Golsan said, "I have to say that bangles are really cheap, four for only half a rupee."

Misri's father said, "Golsan, did you just arrive?"

"Yes, I thought there might be some work to do here. What can I do? I feel I should come here every day, but I have my own chores at home. There aren't many days left before the *Shraddha* ceremony."

Hearing Golsan's unperturbed response, Misri glanced at her in surprise.

"*Shraddha* is in four days. The shopping and everything else has to be done. If you don't do it, who will?"

"Yes, I'll be sure to do it. I've always done it."

After her father had gone, Misri took her eyes away from Golsan's face, thinking that if their eyes met she wouldn't be able to take her eyes away, and she would be caught in a trap.

Golsan said, "In that case..."

Misri became very tense, and her heart seemed suddenly to fall.

"Why—speak," Golsan said.

Misri said in a tearful voice, "Golsan..."

Golsan said nothing, only smiled as she saw Misri's confusion.

Misri said, "Don't upset me!"

Golsan said nothing, and kept watching her, frightening her. Golsan's face seemed very cruel. In no case should she annoy Golsan. She must not speak for fear of making her angry. It seemed to her that she was a fly in Golsan's fist, that if Golsan were to tighten her fist it would mean Misri's certain destruction. Misri said in a calm voice, "How could I go? You tell me."

Golsan thought for a moment and said, "If you don't want to go, don't go. I'm just letting you know."

To Misri it seemed that Golsan's voice had given her an order: "You must go."

She began to scratch a fingernail. Golsan said, "I was just like you at that time—trying to think of whether or not I should go. And one day, I made up my mind and left. What will be, will be."

It seemed to Misri that Golsan was saying out loud what she herself was thinking. She looked at Golsan in surprise. As Misri could not say it wasn't true, Golsan continued to speak. Golsan's voice, in those dancing words and the sense of those words, washed over Misri, and whatever Misri wanted to say in response seemed untrue. What Golsan said was that her life was enjoyable now, now all was wonderful. She now felt no trace of that kind of misery. Misri knew that Golsan had three daughters. Her oldest son had become a guard for an office—that also Misri knew. Golsan shivered with gooseflesh whenever she thought of her first husband—he was a boor, a redneck, a fool. He worked in the fields, came home, gobbled up his food, then slept. It was true that they had no shortage of food there. And true, there were ten or twelve *ropanis* of land for farming. Food, however, his not enough—you also need something to wear, and a few other things. She came to the conclusion that there was no hope of getting anything from that husband. Golsan was unable to do hard work, so she could not break up the clods in the fields. She had grown up in comfort, but her husband did not understand that. He had no idea of how to love. To him, whatever his parents told him was right.

It seemed to Misri that Golsan had opened her mind and was testing these reminiscences. Misri kept trying to say, "It's not like that," but she couldn't manage to speak. Golsan laughed so much her back teeth showed. "As soon as that first husband walked into the room he would pounce on me like a tiger, and after he finished, he slept like Kumbhakarna!"

Misri could not laugh. Golsan covered her back teeth with her lips, but in Misri's eyes the smiling teeth still danced. Golsan went on to say that her first husband didn't know a bean about how to love. Her present husband is head servant in an important official's house. She said angrily, "Since the Congress Party came and took away the government's power, it's hard to get payoffs. That's caused me some trouble. Otherwise, no matter what, he brings me what he's promised. He looks after me very well! No matter what, I am happy. Some have enough food, and some don't, but if there is misery in your heart no matter how much good food you eat, it will still taste like poison!"

Misri's face was solemn. She was lost in thought, and in her face all feelings were sleeping, as if her mental state were far from herself, completely detached, with no connection.

After looking at Misri's face for a moment, Golsan said, "But whatever happens, dear, if you live with the one you love, even hell seems like heaven. Even if you have a heavenly life with someone you don't love, it's like sleeping on thorns."

Misri just glanced at Golsan, and gave no reply. After a moment, she had the impression that those two eyes were those of her husband, and the eyes of that Hiraman were trying to sink into them. Suddenly she had the impression that her husband was victorious and his pitiful eyes were looking at her meekly. Whatever happens, she must survive, must make a decision, and must say something to Golsan. She looked at Golsan and as she looked at her with all the courage she could muster, in a moment she became cold. She said, "Golsan, don't tell anyone about this, all right?"

Just as she spoke, she felt that she hadn't wanted to say this to Golsan, she hadn't wanted to say this. Golsan said, "Ah! Why would I say anything? What need would I have to say anything?"

After Golsan had left, it seemed to Misri that she hadn't said what she had wanted to say. Rather, she had said something else, which Golsan, relieved, had taken away. As she sat, she began to be assailed by doubts. Maybe Golsan had already whispered to someone about the relationship between her and Hiraman. Golsan could not keep this to herself. Misri's doubts grew. It seemed possible that for some time Golsan had spread gossip. Deep inside, she felt suffocated with fear. Yesterday she had not been aware, but today she was. Yesterday her neighbors all around were looking at her, and the shopkeepers along the road were likewise watching her. That look was not the same as before; it was a different kind of look.

For some time she felt pained, and then she felt her suspicions were groundless. No, all those who were looking at her were looking as they always had. Otherwise, why should that Sanumaya across the way have said, "Have you had your meal?" as usual. Thinking this, she felt relieved. But then, thinking again, she thought that if Golsan hadn't said anything yet, she would after a few days. Misri would give her the new sari she had bought, to shut her up. If the sari alone didn't do it, she would giver her a ring. If her mother said, "Where is the ring?" she would say, "Oh, I must have lost it on the street!"

In the evening, Golsan came again. When Misri saw her, her heart began to beat wildly. She wanted to avoid her and run away. When Golsan took her hand, she recoiled and felt stunned. Golsan said, "So—when will you go?"

Misri, without giving a reply, went automatically to her room. Golsan followed her. Misri, unable to give a reply, sat down. Golsan was still waiting for her to say something. Misri felt completely helpless and tears began to fall from her eyes.

Golsan said, "In that case..."

Misri wiped her tears with the edge of her sari and, trying to smile, said, "Golsan..."

After waiting for some time, Golsan said, "Tell me!"

Misri, snapping back as if returning from the unknown, said in the same voice as before, "Say to your master..."

"What shall I say?"

"How can I go, Golsan? Tell me. How could I go? What would he say?"

"Who?"

Misri, abashed, looked at Golsan; she felt ashamed. How could she answer the question "Who?" with the answer "My husband"? Quickly, she said, "My father. My mother." She saw Golsan smile, and felt defeated. "Tell me. Don't I need my father, my mother? Won't everyone curse me? You tell me."

She looked at Golsan, wringing her hands pitiably. Golsan giggled.

"You are laughing!" Misri sighed.

"If I didn't laugh, what could I do, seeing what a state you're in! What is there to fear? Your father and mother will be angry for two or three days. They'll never see you again, they'll say. Later: 'She's our daughter.' Their love will return. Do you fear the laughter of others? People talk, even if you don't do anything. It doesn't really matter—even if they talk, they'll only talk for three or four days. Then they'll get tired of it, and be quiet. And then they'll forget whose wife you were, who you were—they'll all forget."

Misri looked at Golsan as if she'd received a sudden shock. She looked as if she wanted to say, "In that case, everyone will forget that I was first his wife; in that case he also will forget that I had been his wife."

"Later, you, too, will forget," said Golsan, as if she could read her thoughts.

"I, too?" Misri said with a sigh.

For some time the two of them were silent. "He won't forget. He can't forget." Misri thought of her husband's helpless eyes.

"So when will you go? Tell me! The master is tormenting me, and won't leave me in peace," said Golsan.

"I don't know, I don't know!" Misri said irritably. When Golsan said nothing, she said forcefully, "I'm not going!"

"In that case, I'll tell him that. Why should I care?" Golsan got up. She reached the stairs. Misri became frightened when she saw Golsan walking so purposefully. In a gentle voice she called, "Golsan."

Golsan returned and looked at Misri. As Misri said nothing further, she said, "Why did you call me?"

Misri, however, hesitated for a moment. What she was trying to say did not fit into the words she was thinking. After a moment, she said slowly, "Tell your master..."

Golsan waited a moment and asked, "What shall I say? Tell me quickly!"

After a long time Misri said, "Tell him to forget me. I am a married woman."

"I've told him that many times, but he says once you fall in love, love doesn't die!" Golsan said, making a powerful effort to stop smiling.

Misri looked at Golsan with astonishment, as if she had been speaking to Hiraman instead of Golsan.

"So..." she stopped and became silent.

"So, when will you go?" Golsan asked.

Misri continued to look, stunned, at Golsan.

Golsan said, "Day after tomorrow? After three days?"

Misri shook her head in a way which could have been yes or no.

"In that case, in four days!"

Misri as if magnetized, shook her head.

"Ah! *Shraddha* is in four days!" said Golsan.

Misri suddenly remembered that on the day of *Shraddha* her husband was coming. As if making fun of herself, as if equally making fun of everyone, she smiled and said, "Yes!"

"You'll go on that day? Don't lie!"

Misri, as if mocking herself and everyone, said, "Yes!"

"In that case, I'll tell that to the master."

Some time had passed since Golsan left, and Misri felt very agitated. She thought of how Golsan had left with the impression that she was going with Hiraman; she had meant she was going with her husband. She left her room. Now she must tell Golsan—no, she must say to Golsan before she spoke to Hiraman, "I said that I was going with my husband to his house. I didn't say I was going with Hiraman." She ran to the kitchen.

Golsan was not in the kitchen. Her mother was sorting the dal and her sister-in-law was cleaning the rice. Misri stood watching her mother and sister-in-law. Her husband would come on the day of *Shraddha*. It would be like meeting him for the first time, and she would be freed from all troubles. She would go with her husband to her house and would never come back here to her parents' house. There was so much misery and trouble here.

Her mother said, "Golsan was downstairs, wasn't she? Where is she? I need to send her out to do something."

Misri doubtfully examined her mother, but was relieved to see no inkling of suspicion in her mother's face. She said, "I don't know. Where could she have gone?"

Immediately it occurred to her that this would be her last meeting with her husband, and at that meeting the two of them would be separated. She hurriedly left the kitchen and went downstairs. She had to meet with Golsan today and had to say, "I meant, I must go with my husband to my home—how could I go with Hiraman?"

That day, Golsan did not come back. At night, when Misri was trying to sleep it seemed that Golsan had already told Hiraman and that maybe Hiraman would be overjoyed. What a mistake I've made, she thought, turning over again. She must remind Golsan—she turned onto her other side—she must make Golsan understand that she said she must return home with her husband. If Golsan didn't believe her and didn't pay attention, she would get angry and say, "Look, I'll tell my mother and father." If even that did not frighten her, and Golsan threatened to make noise, she would give Golsan the ring from her finger.

That night, something like sleep came over her at about midnight, although it wasn't really sleep; it was like drowsiness, and yet not like drowsiness. At that time she heard the sound of her husband's sigh—"Truthfully, are you going?" She woke up completely. There was no one in the room, and she was alone. The whole room was completely silent, and the house and the entire neighborhood were quiet. It seemed to her that his sigh full of misery was spreading throughout the whole house. She herself sighed like that, and said, "I'm not going. For sure, I'm not going."

In the morning when she woke up, what had happened did not exist, and what had not happened, did. The events of the day and night before had dimmed. Only the low sound of her own sigh came to her as if from a distance. "I'm not going. For sure, I'm not going." She rubbed her eyes and opened them. The corner window of the house opposite was enveloped in sunlight. The sun fell on the night's dew around that house, and the dew was changing to steam. For a long time she looked at that house without being engrossed in it, detached, as if she had formed the habit of looking at it.

She moved quickly away from the window. The events of the day before came back to her. Oh! She wondered how she could have said to Golsan that she would go. She must speak to Golsan today, even though it was late. She went upstairs; Golsan was not there. She went down to her father's room—Golsan was not there either. She went up to the roof terrace, and Golsan was not there either. She went down to the ground floor; no, Golsan was not there either. Golsan had not come. So Misri was helpless, and went to the kitchen, where she sat down to sort the rice offerings for the gods.

As she was sorting the offerings, she looked up and then all about. To her that kitchen, the pots, everything, looked like a dream. Sister-in-law was at the hearth cooking the rice, her face inflamed from the fire, as in a dream. Her own sorting of the offerings for the gods also seemed like a dream. The offering grains were dancing on the plate. The chosen grains mixed together with the broken ones that had been set aside.

After a long time, she understood that her mother had asked her to bring a shawl from her room. She got up and walked as if sleep-walking. She went downstairs to fetch the shawl, where her father said, "Misri, ask your mother what we still need to get for the day after tomorrow. I'll go now to buy them. What is she doing upstairs? Send her downstairs. I won't have time during the day."

Misri was in a trance. She only understood "I won't have time." She took the kitchen tray again to the kitchen and started to sort the offerings, then suddenly remembered—she had forgotten to bring the shawl. She got up and ran downstairs.

"Where is your mother?" her father asked.

Taking the shawl, Misri said hurriedly, "I'll send her."

While she was going out of the room, she saw Golsan grinning at her, and she was struck dumb with terror.

Golsan said, "I just arrived."

Misri watched her, astonished as before, as if she still wanted to comprehend whether Golsan was in a dream or in reality.

Golsan said, in a mysterious manner, "From *there.*"

Misri suddenly woke up. She hurriedly climbed the stairs and entered her own room, where she leaned against the wall.

Golsan followed her into the room and said, "The master was overjoyed!"

Misri still said nothing, and had turned her head away. Golsan said, "Why aren't you saying anything? Why are you shy with me?"

Misri turned to look, and smiled pitiably. Then she said, "Why should I feel shy in front of you, Golsan?"

"Oho! It's late, and your mother called me earlier." Golsan took out a piece of paper from inside her blouse, and said, "Here, take it, this letter. The master wouldn't leave me in peace for a moment. He came to my house to call for me."

The piece of paper fell to the floor. Misri tensed up as she saw the paper. She was unable to say whatever she tried to say, as Golsan was gone in a flash. The piece of paper bearing the letter blew back and forth, then flipped over. Hearing the sound of someone descending the stairs, Misri rapidly picked it up. The sound on the stairs slowly faded away. Misri saw Hiraman's handwriting on the piece of paper. The collected letters were saying, "You say you are coming—there is no way to express my happiness. Get ready the day after tomorrow, the night after *Shraddha* is finished, and come to meet me. I'll be waiting in a car at the turn in the road."

Misri, surprising herself, giggled. "I'll be waiting in a car at the turn in the road" she read again, and laughed again in the same way. It seemed to her that everything was mocking her. To make fun of herself, she said, "In that case, you are going?"

"I am going, and who cares!" she answered herself.

"So go, with the one you love," she said mockingly to herself. "That hoodlum will give you clothes, will give you jewelry. You won't have to work. There will be plenty of servants. You'll live like a queen—what fun it will be. You don't need your mother or father. Even if they cut off your nose, you won't have a care. How lucky you are!"

Misri again laughed this strange laugh.

"That hoodlum will be standing, waiting, at that turn in the road. You will go, looking everywhere, all around. He will reach out his hand to you. You will sit in the car. Zoom! The car will fly, you will fly away. That hoodlum will speak in the car. Do you know what you will say?"

"I don't know." Acting, she answered herself.

"Misri-sister! Misri-sister!" Sister-in-law called from upstairs. "Your mother says come upstairs!"

Misri hesitated a moment to give a response. Sister-in-law's voice was also mocking her. She hid the letter inside her blouse, and felt the cold paper on her breast. A sharp tingle pervaded her whole body. She became serious and she stood leaning against the wall, exhausted.

Upstairs, Golsan was helping to sort the vegetables. When she saw Misri, she was serious for a moment, and then showed her teeth as she smiled privately. Misri turned her head away in disgust.

However, she had something to say to Golsan. She turned her head to give a sign to Golsan with her eyes. But at that time it seemed that she had already said everything. Golsan again showed her back teeth, and smiled in her own way. Misri's entire body suddenly burned with hatred, and she turned her head and left.

After some time it happened that she and Golsan were face to face in privacy. Golsan said, "You are satisfied, right?"

Misri opened her mouth to say something. Again it was as if she forgot everything, as if all had been said. Misri's older brother was coming up the stairs. Misri quickly ran away. Golsan said to her brother, "Master, whenever I see you, you always look so young!"

Misri's face twisted with hatred; how could Golsan be joking at such a time?

All day Golsan did housework here and there in the house. Misri wanted to be alone with her and wanted to talk with her, but when it looked as they might be alone together, she got frightened and ran away. Suddenly she would feel swamped by a wave of anxiety, and then just as suddenly calmness would return and she would feel weary.

At night, she was alone in her room. It seemed to her that her room was completely filled up with a sigh. She took out the letter and read it. The handwriting in the letter also spoke with a sigh, it seemed. Tired, she held the letter in her hand. After a moment, like the day before yesterday, she heard that voice of her husband sighing, "Are you really going?" She looked all around. It seemed to her that her eyes met the helpless eyes of her husband. She cried.

After a while, she thought that the next day she would give Golsan a clear response, and would say "I'm not going." If Golsan still tried to wheedle or flatter her, still tried to make her feel helpless, or didn't leave her alone, Misri would cry out, screaming. Then, the day after tomorrow on the day of *Shraddha,* she would go home with her own husband. There also, if that Hiraman came to bother her as before, she would pressure her husband to leave Nepal and go work in some foreign country. Not long ago her husband had said something about getting transferred to the Terai; she would ask him to do that.

In the morning, when she awoke, the sun had already been up for some time. She awoke with a clear head, as if refreshed, and taking her time she washed and went into the kitchen. But when she reached the kitchen, she became frightened like yesterday, and she turned around and left. Golsan had been there talking with her mother since early morning.

Again, just like yesterday, she felt an incomprehensible wave of anxiety. After some time, Golsan came to her, smiled, and said, "I'm just going to give the young master an invitation for tomorrow."

Misri looked at Golsan, dumbfounded.

Pretending to be vexed, Golsan said, "All right, in any case I have to invite your husband. 'Tomorrow, come early,' I'll say."

Misri stood stock-still, like a statue.

Golsan laughed, as if at a great joke. "Right? I'll have to say that!"

After Golsan left, the sight of her laughing face remained trapped in Misri's eyes. Later, she felt hurt and very angry; Golsan would later speak with her husband with the same mocking laugh. After a moment, as if defeated, she said to herself, "Poor thing, what does he know?"

"I'm not going. I'm not going!" she sighed. She would cry and say to Golsan, "I'm not going!"

At that time, she heard her mother's loud voice calling, "Daughter-in-law!"

Suddenly Misri felt the same wave of anxiety spread over her as yesterday, and she confusedly paced back and forth in the room. When her eye fell on the house opposite, she sat down, crouching in terror. Over there, Hiraman was watching from the window. For a long time the image of that house opposite danced in her eyes and she couldn't get up.

It seemed to Misri that Golsan had just left when she returned again. Golsan had returned and was looking at her. Her face was filled with some kind of laughter, as if it were a great joke, and she said, "The young master, your husband, will come! And why not?"

Misri felt that there was nothing more that she had to say. She felt that all her thoughts, all her wisdom, all her power or reasoning had become nothing. She looked at Golsan with emotionless eyes and her eyelids closed by themselves like a machine. After that, she walked like a shadow throughout the house, and her whole body moved mechanically.

She no longer had the strength for astonishment when she saw her mother talking with Golsan in a natural manner, as if some extraordinary thing were not about to happen. Even the sight of her mother's simplicity and ignorance did not surprise her.

When she was alone with Golsan, Golsan whispered, "You have to get your things ready!"

She looked at Golsan without comprehension. Golsan said irritably, "What are you looking at? Get your clothes ready—there will be no free time tomorrow!"

"Yes." Misri came to, and confusedly went to her room.

"Yes, I have to get things ready, things I need to take," she said to herself, and opened her trunk. Then she heard in her mind a helpless, quiet cry. "No, no!' However, she opened the trunk and began to turn over the folded clothes one by one. There, different colors, different printed designs, different clothes—*toprel* blouses, colorful printed shawls, printed dotted blouses, mercerized dhotis, and Georgette saris. They all dazzled her eyes. Suddenly, it was as if she had forgotten everything. She sat leaning against the chest and asked herself, "Why? Why am I gathering my clothes together?"

Just then, her younger brother Ramesh came in and said, "Father asked if you had already sent out for the spices and herbs."

Misri did not reply. Ramesh said, "Why don't you say anything? What are you thinking? Did you already send for them?"

Misri said curtly, "We already sent for them."

But immediately she sighed, and said, "I don't know."

"Why? What are you doing? Where are you going that you need to change clothes?"

"I am going," Misri said with a sigh.

"Where?"

Misri said confusedly, "Nowhere. Tomorrow I'm going, right?" She hesitated again and said, "No, not tomorrow, day after tomorrow."

She closed the chest. Ramesh went out.

"Where? Where am I going?" she said again to herself.

When she left her room she met Golsan, who was bringing in a pot of water. Golsan said quietly in her ear, "Is everything ready? Tomorrow everything will be in a state of confusion. I'll take everything today."

"No need!" said Misri, with a trembling voice.

Golsan looked at her sharply and said, "In that case, tomorrow for sure?"

Misri shook her head yes. Golsan said, "No matter what, you must pack today. Who knows what will happen tomorrow."

"You must pack today." For a long time Golsan's words echoed in Misri's ears. Misri mechanically went into her room again, and as if under a spell sat down to open the chest. Again she hesitated in the midst of all those colorful clothes. She leaned against the chest like before and asked herself, "Where?"

Hiraman will be standing at the corner, leaning against the car. Then? Empty of thought, she looked at all the various kinds of clothes.

That evening, claiming she had a headache, she went into her room and closed the door. Golsan's voice could be heard regularly, as if coming from the house's bottomless depths, mixed with the voice of her mother. Again, momentarily, many voices were talking together about the preparations for *Shraddha* the next day. Those voices, pressing one upon the other, suffocated her.

Her mother came to say, "Eat a little rice. Tomorrow there will be so much work. But you..."

Misri only looked at her mother's shadow. And slowly she looked at her mother's feet. Those feet were tapered, white, shapely. She looked at those feet as if magnetized.

"Why not eat just a little? You just have a headache, you don't have a fever, right?"

Misri obediently said, "All right" gently, and got up.

She was eating rice. How could the mouthfuls go down her throat? She did not feel capable of thinking. Her whole body felt subdued, dull, and defeated. Her sister-in-law said, "Shall I give you some dal?" and it seemed to Misri that her voice was filled with hatred. Yes, she was hateful and she had no capability or right to oppose that hatred. She finished eating her rice without looking at anyone.

When Misri reached her room, she wrapped herself in her quilt to sleep, but sleep did not come. The night had become motionless, as if stuck, and at the same time ran very swiftly. It seemed to her that she was running away alone, through woods, jungle, hills and to the top of the white Himalayan peaks she could see from the terrace. Then the night would seem motionless, and she would see herself wrapped in her quilt, sleeping.

In the morning, when she awoke, she became aware of her body. She looked at her hands with wonder: she had survived, she hadn't died. She laughed a little to think that her mother and father and everyone in the house could still make some commotion. She automatically opened the window; that house opposite was still there. It hadn't disappeared. The sun was on that house just the same, just as before.

Golsan tried not to let on to others that she had come to see Misri. Golsan said hurriedly, "Is everything ready?"

Misri only looked at Golsan without blinking; Golsan, too, remained as usual. Golsan hurriedly repeated, "Is everything ready, I said."

"I haven't yet got things ready," said Misri timidly.

"Why not?"

"I'll get them ready," said Misri in a defeated voice.

Just then a man arrived with a load of vegetables. "Where should I put these?"

Golsan said angrily, "Don't leave them here! Don't you know better? Take them upstairs to the kitchen!"

Misri smiled a little. Golsan said irritably, "Why are you smiling? Get your things ready!"

At the same time, someone called, "Golsan! Golsan!" Golsan cursed and said, "How many times are they going to call me? Get ready, eh? I'm going."

The meat for the feast arrived. For *Shraddha*, the lower floor was being given a fresh coat of cow dung. The Brahman priest had arrived, and *Shraddha* had begun. Her mother rebuked Ramesh for not doing anything, and she handed Misri a copper tray. "Why are you daydreaming? Do I have to do everything myself?"

As she was bringing the copper tray down the stairs, Golsan asked, "Have you got everything ready?"

Misri said nothing as she went downstairs. Golsan quickly came after her. Misri hurriedly descended.

Fearing she might meet Golsan, Misri was afraid to be alone, but she also wanted to run away from this big crowd of people.

Shraddha was finished. Misri's mother called her to take part in the worship of the ancestral offering. Misri went there and received the offering in her hand, and it seemed that all her ancestors together were staring at her.

As her father was presenting her an offering of a *tika* and a coin, she dropped the coin. Misri quickly picked it up and went out.

She was afraid not only of loneliness, but also of the large crowd. Golsan managed to meet with her anyway and said, "You've still not made things ready?"

After staring at Misri for a time, Golsan said, "Go, comb your hair. I'll get things ready myself."

Obediently, Misri went to her own room. Golsan said, "Give me the key."

Misri gave the key to Golsan without saying anything. Golsan said, "Go! Please comb your hair."

Misri went in front of the mirror and sat down to comb her hair. When she saw her own face in the mirror, she was surprised to see how thin she had become in two or three days, how faded and forlorn her face looked.

Golsan said, "Shall I take out the Kashmiri shawl?"

It seemed to Misri that she had seen a face like her own in a photo somewhere.

Golsan said, "You'll need your Kashmiri shawl in these cold months." Yes, Misri thought she looked like a hag in the Mahadev marriage procession. She giggled a little.

Not getting a reply, Golsan said, "It seems as if you need almost everything."

Outside, Misri's elder brother was calling, "Sanuman! Sanuman!" as he climbed the stairs. Golsan said confusedly, "It's not possible to pick and choose. One or two blouses, one or two shawls, and two or three saris will be enough."

As Misri combed her hair, running the comb through her hair with her hand, she looked at herself steadily. Outside, there was much commotion. Golsan picked up two blouses, two shawls, and three saris; whatever her hand happened to touch she picked up and put in a bundle. Taking a long breath as if she had gained a victory, she said, "Finished! Now what is to be done?"

"Oho! What are you doing? Haven't you finished combing your hair yet?" she said, looking at Misri.

Misri was very slowly moving the comb through her hair. Golsan said, "All right, comb your hair, eh?" and left. Misri stopped combing and again looked steadily at her face. Then, she threw the comb on the floor, and, laying the mirror down flat, she got up. She would not comb her hair; she wouldn't need make-up.

By that time, the tantric rites were finished, and Misri's father, mother, and everyone else had gone downstairs. It was past two o'clock. Misri also sat with her father and their relatives to eat the banquet. While she was eating, Golsan frequently came inside to look at her doubtfully. After everyone had finished eating, Misri suddenly felt a wave of anxiety—what if her husband did not come today; what if he were sick and couldn't come?

Four, five, then six o'clock came. All the remaining guests had also finished eating the banquet. Her husband had not yet come. What if he didn't come! She must see her husband, must speak with her husband. She must look at him in his pitiful eyes and speak with him. For that reason she was waiting for him at the *Shraddha* ceremonies.

She leaned against the door of the kitchen, thinking. It seemed to her that if she bathed in the depths of her husband's eyes, she would die in peace.

A man carrying a load of food scolded her: "What are you doing here? Why are you blocking the way?"

Misri went away. While she was on the stairs, Golsan pulled on the edge of her shawl. Misri turned around and looked at Golsan dumbly. She felt that in a flash she had returned to the same place she had already been liberated from.

Golsan said, "You didn't comb your hair at all. You didn't put on any jewelry or makeup."

Misri said, "I'll not comb my hair."

"Why? Are you going like that?"

"Yes." She looked helplessly at Golsan.

Someone came, and Golsan left. It seemed to Misri that her own voice was not really her voice. That "Yes" was not her voice.

It was seven o'clock, and her husband had still not come. She had waited for many days, for years and years, from a previous birth she had waited for that husband, and he still hadn't come.

Misri sat near the stairs on the top floor. Every time there was a footstep on the stairs she stopped her breath to listen. Then her heart began to beat wildly. She heard the sound of her husband's footsteps on the stairs. She got up and went to sit by the window on the top floor. The sound of her husband's steps went into her father's room below and disappeared. Golsan came to stand close to Misri. Misri jumped, and ran away to her own room; from deep inside, her soul cried out, "O Bhagwan! O Bhagwan!"

After some time Golsan came into her room. For a while she finished some small tasks, then said, "After living together for some time, being together, and walking the same road, it turns out it is difficult to stop caring."

Misri stared at Golsan, wanting to comprehend that she was still the same Golsan. Golsan said, "A person who doesn't love is not human."

Now Misri had the impression that this Golsan was not the same Golsan as before. Misri gently asked, "Where is he? Is he downstairs?"

"He's gone upstairs."

Misri jumped from the room and quickly went up the stairs. Then she stood stock-still in the door of the kitchen.

Inside, her husband had begun to eat. She was astonished; that face was as before. She looked: that face was indeed as before, but it seemed he had become thinner. Those eyes were pitiable. She watched: those kind eyes were speaking with her elder brother, laughing a little. Now again, he was pitiable as before.

"Why are you standing out here? If you want to watch so much, you can come inside," said her sister-in-law.

Misri did try to go inside, but stopped. She looked dumbly as she saw, there with her husband, her elder brother's friend, who was also eating. Again she stood stock-still. Now, her husband had become serious and was saying something to her elder brother.

As they looked, Misri's eyes seemed to behold a dream. She was not now the Misri of the present;

now she was the Misri of her marriage year. This was not the day of *Shraddha*—it was the day of her marriage. Her husband was not the husband who was now eating this feast of *Shraddha*; it was the husband of her wedding day, who was shyly eating his food. This was the *Shraddha* of the year of her marriage, not today's *Shraddha*. For that reason, she was not sitting here to look, she was sitting below in her room, listening to the accounts of her cousins, how shy he had been to look at them, how he picked out the pieces of meat, how he mixed his *chiura*. This feast was not today's feast; it was the year of her marriage.

Right then, Golsan pulled her away. In a flash, her husband, who was eating, was lost to her view. In a moment, she had reached the stairs.

"He has been waiting at the corner for some time," said Golsan softly.

Golsan again gave her a push. Misri left the kitchen and went downstairs. Golsan said, "I'll carry your bundle of clothes. Now, put on your shoes."

Golsan put the shoes in front of her. Misri unconsciously put on her shoes. Golsan took her hand and pulled her. She reached the lowest floor.

"Don't be afraid—I'm here," Golsan said.

In a flash, as if lost in a dream, Misri left the house.

PBH

OTHER NOVELS FROM PILGRIMS BOOK HOUSE

CONFESSION

by Kavita Ram Shrestha
Translated by Larry Hartsell

Boldly written and controversial, this powerful translation is available for the first time in the English language. The Nepali characters of a sick woman, a dwarf and a whore portray frustrated people which society creates but then turns into objects of hatred. Although it is a story of opposition to society's values, it is, as the author says, "a story that exists in all places, times and personalities." Introduction by Krishnachandra Singh.

75 pages. Paperback. **US $ 4.00**
ISBN. 81-7303-033-2. Shipping: Sea/Air $1.00/$3.00

KHAIRINI GHAT

by Shankar Koirala
Translated by Larry Hartsell

After having lost himself for ten years in Calcutta, a weary traveller returns to his native village in the hills of Nepal to cope with political and social changes. Attempting to regain his former status, he resists the temptations of village women and manages the affairs of village life. It is an evocative narrative which provides a rare glimpse of rural Nepal in the recent past that is slowly disappearing. "This small sensuous novel...packed with action...has all the ingredients of a best seller"—*The Rising Nepal.*

101 pages. Fiction. Paperback
US $4.50 ISBN. 81-7303-041-1
Shipping: Sea/Air $1.00/$3.00

GUESTS IN THIS COUNTRY: A DEVELOPMENT FANTASY

by Greta Rana

Becky Sidebottom, a recent university graduate, lands her first job as a Junior Programme Officer for an international aid agency in the third world state of Lapalistan. An innocent abroad, Becky quickly learns the ropes and gets caught up in a maelstrom of espionage, counter-revolution, romance, pregnancy and tennis matches. This humorous but thought-provoking novel is a biting spoof about the new colonialism of development aid which benefits admin-istrators and local elites more than the poor.

365 pages. Paperback
US $ 7.50 Item No: 81 7303 034 0
Shipping: Sea/Air $2.00/$9.00

A CLASSFUL OF GODS AND GODDESSES IN NEPAL

by Ruth Higbie

An American Peace Corps volunteer describes the rewards and frustrations of working as a science teacher in Banepa, a Newar mountain village near Kathmandu. She seeks to understand her Nepali students, colleagues and neighbours by getting involved in the everyday life of the village.

195 pages. Paperback. B&W photographs
US $4.95 Item No: 023 Shipping: $1.00/$3.00

These and other fine titles may be ordered directly. Credit card orders accepted by fax with card number, expiration date and signature. Request our free publication catalogue.

PILGRIMS BOOK HOUSE
P.O. Box 3872, Kathmandu, Nepal.
Fax: 977-1-424943. E-mail: info@pilgrims.wlink.com.np